The Secret of the Sealed Room

Also by Bailey MacDonald

Wicked Will

THE
SECRET OF THE
SEALED ROOM

BAILEY MacDONALD

Aladdin

NEW YORK LONDON TORONTO SYDNEY

ALADDIN
An imprint of Simon & Schuster Children's Publishing Division
1230 Avenue of the Americas, New York, NY 10020
First Aladdin hardcover edition October 2010
Copyright © 2010 by Brad Strickland
For information about special discounts for bulk purchases, please contact
Simon & Schuster Special Sales at 1-866-506-1949 or business@simonandschuster.com.
The Simon & Schuster Speakers Bureau can bring authors to your live event. For more information or to book an event contact the Simon & Schuster Speakers Bureau at 1-866-248-3049 or visit our website at www.simonspeakers.com.
The text of this book was set in Hoefler Text.
Manufactured in the United States of America 0810 FFG

2 4 6 8 10 9 7 5 3 1

Full CIP data for this book is available from the Library of Congress.
ISBN 978-1-4169-9760-3
ISBN 978-1-4169-9762-7 (eBook)

✺ One ✺

*What signifies your patience, if you can't find it
when you want it?*
—*Poor Richard's Almanac*

My name is Patience, but I have little of that with all those in Boston who keep telling me what a bad girl I am. When I learned my letters, the very first sentence I could read proved a harsh and scolding one: *In Adam's fall, we sinned all.* In church of a Sunday when the parson preaches about the sins and failings of women, I would swear he gazes straight at me with a stern, disapproving look. And of course Mrs. Worth, to whom my father bound me as a servant when my mother died, always assured me that I am a lazy, sullen, disobedient, and wicked wretch, destined to come to an evil end.

But let me begin at the beginning, on a September day in the year of our Lord 1721. Mrs. Worth had rung her bell for me early, before the sun had risen, and I found her groaning in her bed. "Child," she said, "run and fetch Moll Bacon, and hurry!"

"I must dress—," I began, only to be cut short by her angry words: "Go, I tell you! Go, and hurry!"

Still I dressed hastily, then set out running from the Worth house, on its low hill overlooking the Roxbury Road, right down Orange Street and so to Newbury Street and then into the still-sleeping heart of Boston. Mists crept through the streets like silent cats, gray in the dimness before dawn. Hardly any faint yellow lights showed, but I knew the way right well: along Marlborough and Cornhill streets south of the Common, then a sharp turn onto Water Street, with its narrow shops and dark, looming warehouses. A lonely rooster crowed somewhere, and then another answered him, and another. Dogs barked as I hurried through the damp and the dark, feeling the wet cobbles slippery beneath the thin soles of my worn-out shoes, shivering in the coolness of the early-September morning.

The fishermen were up already, of course. Far ahead, down toward the Long Wharf, I could see the reddish glows of their lanterns on the face of the night. I even heard a distant fisherman's gruff, growling voice singing the words of a doleful old ballad:

"As I walked forth one summer's day
To view the meadows green and gay,
A pleasant bower I espied
Standing fast by the riverside,
And in't a maiden I heard cry:
Alas! Alas! There's none e'er loved as I."

Having no time to listen, I hurried on until I came to a great warehouse that smelled strongly of fish, and I began to count the buildings beyond it, two, three, four, and there I turned into the pitch-dark, narrow alley that leads back around the corner to Moll Bacon's cottage. Though small, it nestles in a neat and clean yard blooming with little herb and flower gardens, and the white paint on the house and its picket fence is smart and fresh-looking, or at least it is in sunlight. In the darkness both seemed to glow a pearly gray.

Early though it was, as I approached Moll Bacon's cottage, I glimpsed candlelight through a window, and when I rapped at the door, the old midwife opened it at once. She was already dressed, as if she really had the second sight that some in Boston whispered fearfully about. "What is it, girl?" she asked gruffly.

I did not flinch from her, though she had a dark face sharp as an Indian tomahawk, all sharp angles and cutting edges, and beneath her heavy black brows her scowl made her look as fierce as the old Abenaki warrior she claimed as her grandfather. "My mistress wants you," I said.

She grunted and tilted her head. "You are the Martin girl. You belong to Abedela Worth."

"I belong to myself," I said with as much spirit as I could, meeting her dark-eyed gaze. "But I work for Mrs. Worth."

She laughed then, one sharp, gruff bark, and she turned half away from me as she reached for something—a large basket, I saw. "Come, then, Patience Martin, and let's see to the woman you work for."

Moll did not lock the door, and answering my glance rather than my words she said, "None in Boston would dare come in without my permission. Fast walking will warm us, girl. Carry this."

I took the basket, which was covered with a calico cloth and as heavy as a load of stone, but no answer did I make. Only a month or so earlier, when Mrs. Worth first suspected that she was with child, had I met this strange woman. That very first time she had curtly told me not to call her Mistress Bacon, or even Goody Bacon, as some of the older people did. "Moll's my name, and that's what you shall call me," she had said. Since that first time, Moll Bacon had come to the house often, sometimes two or three times each week, for Mrs. Worth was having a hard time of it. I should have felt sorry for her, a poor widow woman whose husband was three months drowned and herself four months gone in pregnancy. I could not feel much sympathy for her, though, with my own father dead in the same ship as her husband, and my future so clouded, and her hand so hard and so ready to slap me for any small failing on my part. Perhaps my lack of compassion was another measure of my badness.

We trotted along side by side in the slowly growing light of dawn. Moll spoke little, but once she suddenly asked, for no reason that I could see, "How old are you, girl?"

"Fourteen last month," I replied, panting. I understood that Moll Bacon herself was no more than forty-five, though I thought she looked a good twenty years older, and she made a good pace of it, so that I had to scurry to keep up, never getting a chance to catch my breath. We reached the house, and I saw lights in the downstairs windows. The chickens were awake now, murmuring and scratching about the backyard. I started toward them, for Mrs. Worth was very strict about my never coming in through the front door, but that opened as Moll and I stepped into the yard. A tall, thin, gray man beckoned impatiently for us to come in that way: Mr. Richard Worth, Mrs. Worth's brother-in-law. He was past fifty—Mrs. Worth's husband, Jared, his older brother, had been sixty when he drowned—and he had a sharp, waspish manner. He and his son, David, were Mrs. Worth's nearest neighbors. "She's very ill," snapped Mr. Richard. "You'd best hurry." He turned his gaze on me. "Don't stand there with your basket! Go with her. Make yourself useful!"

I gave him a barely polite nod of my head, and together with Moll I hurried up the stair to the second-floor bedroom, where my mistress lay moaning dolefully.

Mrs. Worth, her already thin cheeks sunken, lay back on her feather pillow, her brown hair hidden beneath her nightcap. Her red-rimmed eyes glittered in anger as we came into the gloomy room. "Why did you take so long?" she demanded in an unnaturally hoarse voice.

"I came as quickly as I could," replied Moll. "Are you in pain?"

"My head is splitting, and my stomach is cramping terribly. I am afraid I might lose the baby."

Moll took the basket from me, then pointed to the fine beeswax candle that Mrs. Worth used to read by at night. "Child, light that for me."

"No," grumbled Mrs. Worth. "It's too expensive to burn idly while there is daylight. Open the curtains instead."

"Yes, ma'am," I said. It did not do to cross her in anything, however small. I drew and tied back the curtains from the room's two windows, and the milky light of early day spilled into the dim bedroom. I could not help thinking that the candle would have given Moll considerably more illumination.

"I need you to take this," Moll said, handing me a small, nearly weightless cloth bag that felt as if it contained dried herbs, "and boil it in a pint of water. When the pot begins to bubble, drop this in, and boil it until you can count to a hundred, slowly—you can count, can't you?"

"Of course I can count!"

"She is a tetchy, forward child," said Mrs. Worth, adding a dismal groan.

Moll ignored her: "Count to a hundred, slowly, and then take the pot off the stove and allow it to steep for a quarter of an hour. Then pour off the tea that is brewed, put it in a mug, and bring it to me. Throw away the bag, for the medicine will have no virtue for a second boiling."

"I understand."

Downstairs Mr. Richard was standing beside a fire he had just lit in the parlor grate, his gray hair untidy as though he had been sweeping his hands through it. "How is my sister-in-law?"

"Moll Bacon is nursing her now, sir. I'm to make a medicinal tea from this." I held up the little cloth bag.

"Don't show it to me! Be about it, then."

I bowed my head, grinding my teeth at his snappish tone. "Yes, sir."

The kitchen stove was dark and cold, of course. I was used to attending to it, though, because Mrs. Worth was so near with a shilling that she refused to hire anyone to help me around the house—though I had heard gossips in the street say that her husband had left her very well set, with not only the house and land but a steady income from his investments in ships and trade. As quickly as I could, I raked out the white and gray ashes from the wood-box into the ash scuttle, then piled in some brown and sharp-scented pine shavings as tinder. Atop that I built a small pyramid of kindling—splints of more pine, which would catch easy and burn fast—and then, to weigh that down, a few hickory logs. I got the tinderbox and struck fire with it, then set a splinter alight and touched it to the wood shavings until they were burning. The kindling began to crackle, and the fragrant pine sap started to ooze and flow. I put in two more lengths of hickory and closed the wood-box door. The stove top would be hot in a matter of minutes.

While it heated, I went out to the well and drew a pail of fresh water. The hens came clustering around me, wanting to be fed, and the rooster perched on top of the coop, flapped his wings, and crowed piercingly, and I imagined him proclaiming, *Day, it's day, it's day, it's da-a-a-y!* Filled, the water pail was heavy, and I had to use two hands to carry it back to the kitchen, taking care not to splash it out as I waded through the impatient chickens. I used the late Mr. Worth's pint beer mug to measure the water into the cast-iron teapot and then put the pot on to boil. Mr. Richard had come to the doorway. "Child, don't be idle! Make me a bit of breakfast while I wait."

"Yes, sir."

I scrambled two eggs in butter and fried a nice slice of bread. By then the teapot was bubbling, so I dropped in the little cloth bag. Mr. Richard sat at the table and ate the bread and eggs, drinking only water that he dipped from the pail. His brother, Mrs. Worth's husband, had been a sailor and a sea captain, used to drinking pale ale with breakfast and a glass of rum mixed with water with dinner, but Mr. Richard abstained from all alcohol except a little glass of wine now and then. He served as a deacon in the Congregational Church, and I knew full well that he had never approved of his older brother's ways or habits. I stood by the stove with my chin down, murmuring under my breath.

"What are you doing?" he growled at me. "Praying?"

"Counting," I said, skipping from fifty to fifty-two because I had paused to speak.

"Better for you to pray," he muttered. "Where is that son of mine?"

He did not expect me to answer, and so I didn't, simply going on in my count until I whispered "one hundred" to myself and took the kettle off the stove. I went to the parlor to look at the clock. The minute hand stood at six minutes before the hour.

I had time to eat. Back in the kitchen I fried a little piece of bread for myself and cut a small wedge of cheese from the hoop in the pantry. Mr. Richard pushed away from the table and left me alone as he returned restlessly to the parlor. I finished the bread and cheese, then put our dishes and the frying pan into the wash basin.

In the front parlor, where Mr. Richard stood moodily in front of the fire he had built, staring down into it with his hands clasped behind him, I checked the clock again. The minute hand now touched eight minutes after the hour. I waited until it nicked off another minute, and then I went back to the kitchen. As Moll had directed, I poured the tea into the mug—it was a dark greenish-brown liquid, smelling faintly of licorice—and threw the sodden bag of herbs into the slop pail.

Mrs. Worth looked a little calmer when I brought the tea into the bedroom. "Here we are," said Moll. "Drink this down. It will do you good."

"Where is Richard?" asked Mrs. Worth querulously as she struggled to sit up in bed, propped against both of her pillows.

"He is down in the parlor," I told her. "I made breakfast for him."

"You gave him my food?" she demanded with a cross glance. "What did he eat, and how much?"

"Just two eggs and a slice of bread."

"Remember that," she said, shaking a bony finger at me. "He will have to repay me!" She took a little, cautious sip of the tea and made a sour face at the taste of it.

"I should attend to my chores," I said to Moll, in a small voice.

Mrs. Worth drank the rest of the liquid from the mug, making "Gahh!" sounds after each noisy swallow. "Go," Moll said to me. "I don't need you here right now. But boil more water."

I put more water on the stove, went out and fed the chickens, and then came back inside. With part of the heated water I washed and rinsed the dishes. Then I dried and put them away and threw the dishpan of still-steaming water out into the side yard. The sun was well up now, the day breezy, with scudding raggedy gray and white clouds now and then dimming the light. I went on to my other daily chores, dusting and sweeping, scouring the front steps, and so on. Just before noon Mr. Richard told me to go next door to see if his son, David, was home and to tell him to come over if he was.

"Next door," he said, but it was a little walk away, for here the houses were not close-packed, as they were in the heart of town. I tapped on the back door of Mr. Richard's two-story home—a small house only when compared to his brother's three-story one; Mr. Richard said that an earthly mansion was nothing but a sinful vanity that the Lord would punish in due time—and Mr. David answered on my second knock.

He was twenty-two years old, not very tall but thin, like his father, with a head of thick, curly, auburn-brown hair and quick, darting brown eyes. "Patience," he said. "How is my aunt?"

"Sick and in bed, sir," I replied. "Your father asks that you come over."

A pained expression crossed his face. "I'm sorry that she's ill," he told me. Mr. David's voice always sounded strange in my ear. His father had sent him across the

Atlantic Ocean to Cambridge in England to be schooled, and during his four years there he had lost the Boston accent and had picked up a kind of drawling English one. He had returned home only the previous September, and if street gossip were true, he cut quite a figure among the young ladies of Boston—and among those rakish young men who gamble and live riotously in secret—though I try never to listen to such tattling tales. "Is she suffering much?" he asked me.

"I cannot tell," I said. "She said some while ago that her stomach and head were troubling her. Moll Bacon is giving her medicines, though, and now she seems to be resting more easily. Please, sir, your father told me to come and fetch you."

"I'll come with you. Let me change from my slippers."

He went back inside, not asking me in, of course, and a few minutes later he reappeared, wearing thigh-high riding boots, though we were walking only back to the next house. He kept asking me questions on the way, but I had few answers for him. We heard raised voices as we came to the house, Mr. Richard's and Moll's, and Mr. David gave me an appalled glance. We came in through the back door. In the kitchen Moll stood pouring hot water into a basin, and Mr. Richard was loudly saying, "But a real doctor—!"

"I don't think a doctor could do more than I have done," Moll said shortly.

Mr. Richard snorted. "Potions! Tricks!"

"A warm compress for her belly will ease her pain, sir. It is no trick."

"Brews steeped from herbs! Witch's tricks! I tell you, woman, such things are blasphemy!" roared Mr. Richard.

Mr. David stepped forward and said, "Father, please. Mistress Bacon is only trying to help."

Mr. Richard spun where he stood and focused his anger on his son. "There you are at last!"

"I came as soon as—"

"I want none of your idle chatter! You stay here and help if you can. I need to get back home. There are papers and letters I must deal with, and I cannot spend all day here while that woman is giving Abedela physic."

"How is my aunt, Father?"

Moll Bacon said, "Some better, sir. Let me by, please." She pushed passed him, carrying the basin of steaming water and folded towels. A moment later I heard her steps upon the stair.

"May the Lord protect Abedela in the hands of that— that witch!" said Mr. Richard grimly. He sniffed disdainfully and added, "God's will be done, but I pray the Lord might be merciful to my sister-in-law in her illness."

"Amen," said Mr. David softly.

I said nothing at all, stung by Mr. Richard's choice of words. It seemed to me that if Moll Bacon could ease Mrs. Worth's pain and take away her fears, it was just possible that the Lord had chosen Moll to be his healing instrument. It would never have done to put that thought into spoken words, though, not to Mr. Richard, who firmly believed that all women were wicked and that female children such as I were even more so. Instead I went ahead with my chores, certainly not wishing any harm on my mistress, and yet in all truth hoping that she improved for Moll's sake more than for her own.

For I confess I hated the ugly word that Mr. Richard had put to her name. Whatever else Moll Bacon might be, I surely did not think she was a witch.

❧ TWO ❧

Nothing but money is sweeter than honey.
—*Poor Richard's Almanac*

B y three in the afternoon Mrs. Worth had become
considerably more settled and comfortable. I brought
warm water and sponged her, and Moll Bacon prepared
to leave, for she had to attend to other women who were
expecting babies. "Don't go," my mistress said fretfully.
"What if I should need you?"

"Come, aunt," said Mr. David from the doorway. "Father
and I are just next door, and you have Patience to stay with
you."

"What good is she?" fretted Mrs. Worth. "I want Moll
to stay."

"I have to go now," Moll told her, but Mrs. Worth fussed
so much that at last Moll sighed and took something from

her basket. "Look at this," she said. It was a pretty little glass ball, lavender, about the size of a very small chicken's egg. "This is my special eye. Here, I will put it on the mantel." She carefully set the glass orb there. "It will help me watch over you. Rest now."

In the hall she answered my questioning look: "No, Patience, it is just a glass ball, that is all. I cannot really see through it. But if it eases her mind and lets her sleep, it is as good as medicine."

"A little trick," said Mr. David with a chuckle.

Moll nodded and said to me, "Come for me at once if she gets sick again." I saw her out, and by the time I checked on Mrs. Worth again, she lay slumbering, breathing deeply and easily, with no outward sign of pain.

When I told David that his aunt was sleeping peacefully, he took his leave as well. All through the day I had been working, seeing to the chickens, cleaning the house, emptying the ashes into the lye barrel. Like many in Boston, we made our own soap from fat and lye. All these and many other tasks kept me busy. That afternoon, having finished all of my chores—for I worked faster, I found, when Mrs. Worth was not hanging over my shoulder criticizing me—I sat and read for a while in the Bible. We had few books in the house at all, and it was either that or the well-thumbed *New-England Almanac*, which I had all but memorized.

Most girls in my station, bond servants, did not know how to read, but my father had insisted that I learn that, and some arithmetic. He himself had been an Englishman, and at one time he had wished to be a learned man, but poverty had caused him to take up the hard life of a sailor instead. Even so, he had worked his way up from a common landsman to the mate of a fine trading ship, and in time he might have become a captain. I closed the Bible and thought of the time I had left to serve Mrs. Worth. My father had bound me the year my mother passed away, when I was ten, nearly eleven, and now I had just turned fourteen. I had nearly another four years left to be in service. Four long, long, long years.

From time to time I looked in on Mrs. Worth, but I always found her sleeping more or less peacefully in her darkened room. Before leaving, Moll had advised me to "let the poor woman get her sleep out," and so I did not wake her. As the day warmed, I let the fire in the parlor die and then removed the ashes, though I kept a low fire going in the kitchen stove in case Mrs. Worth should wake and demand some food, for she had eaten nothing. The big house felt lonesome, and for the longest time I had only the dreary tick-tock of the parlor clock for company.

At about five in the afternoon, as I sat quietly looking out the kitchen window at the brown chickens scratching and pecking about the backyard, Mrs. Worth's voice startled me so that I jumped about a yard out of my chair: "You wicked, idle girl! Is this how you behave when I am not telling you what to do?"

"I've already finished my work, ma'am—," I began.

"I'm hungry," said Mrs. Worth, walking slowly into the kitchen, keeping one hand on the wall as though for balance, and then slowly settling into a chair. "But my stomach heaves at the thought of any meat. I want a dish of toast and milk, and be quick."

"I shall have to beg some milk of Mr. Richard—"

"Then go and hurry on your way! Useless, lazy wretch!"

Knowing she was ill-natured and grumpy because of the way she felt, I bit back the sharp reply that danced on my tongue, took an earthenware jar that would hold a little over a pint, and hurried over to Mr. Richard's house. His thin, worried-looking cook, Betty Thayer, was glad enough to give me a pint of fresh milk. She was a bond servant like me, though she was in middle life. She did not like to talk about herself, since she had led a sad sort of existence, but I understood that she and her husband, Nathaniel, had a daughter. When the girl, Eliza, was only about six years old,

Mrs. Thayer's husband had run away, deserting them. Betty was left a poor woman with no means of support. In the end, not finding any other employment and having no relatives, Betty had indentured herself to Mr. Richard for fourteen long years and still had several years to serve. I could not help thinking they must seem like an eternity with a sour-natured person like Mr. Richard as her master.

I think because we were both in the same sort of situation, Betty was kind enough to ask about Mrs. Worth's health. I told her she seemed better.

"How does her illness take her?" Betty asked, busying herself pouring the milk.

"She has terrible pains in her head, she says, and she is so sick to her stomach that often she vomits. And she seems weak when she walks."

"Poor woman," Betty said. "There are few people I would wish such suffering on." She glanced quickly toward the hall door, as if fearing someone might hear her. "Here is your milk, dear. Take it to her, and I wish she may like it."

I took the jar, thanked Betty, and then walked as fast as I dared—the milk was too dear to be spilled—back home. With Mrs. Worth complaining bitterly about my slothfulness, I carefully toasted her some bread, crumbled it into a dish of the milk, and gave it to her, together with a pewter spoon. She had me bow my head while she muttered grace, and then she ate almost mechanically, with no great show of appetite.

When she had finished, I took her dishes and put them in the basin to be washed as she hesitantly and with many gasps pushed herself up out of her chair. Slowly, as though still in discomfort, she walked through the house, darting her irritable glances all around, before grudgingly admitting that she could at the moment find nothing more for me to do. She sat restlessly in the parlor, nestled down in her tall armchair, staring moodily into the cold fireplace. She wore her old blue robe over her nightgown.

I had grown used to seeing her in the black clothing of mourning, so in her gown she looked a little strange to me. I must confess I found it galling that she insisted on good mourning clothes for herself, but she allowed me not even a black ribbon to wear to show my own sorrow for my father's passing. She had snappishly told me, "Servants do not mourn!"

We sat in silence for a dreary long time. Only once did we have company, a boy bringing a few shillings to her, the rent for a small shop that her husband had leased out to a man who bought, repaired, and sold old shoes. Mrs. Worth took the money and settled in the parlor, sitting at the little folding desk where her husband had always done the household accounts, and opened the ledger book where she kept a record of income and expenses. Muttering to herself, she added and subtracted. Then she said in a dissatisfied voice, "Richard has not rented the house in Tanner's Lane. I lose good money every day until that is done!"

Still I said nothing. The house she meant was little more than a shack, poorly built and jammed tight against a stinking tannery. It was one of four or five properties that Mr. Worth had bought and rented out, and of them all it was the least desirable, but since Mrs. Worth insisted on charging exactly the same rent for all the houses, whether larger or smaller, in good repair or ruinous, she had made the cost of living in the Tanner's Lane hovel far too high for the poor folk that might consider it.

Mrs. Worth wanted no supper that evening but had me help her up the stairs to her bedroom, where at her direction I changed the bedclothes—there would be a monstrous heap of washing for me to do come Monday, I thought—and lit the candle, for she proposed to read in the Psalms until she fell asleep again. She had a little cloth purse with her that held the money the boy had brought to her, and she had me drag the heavy iron strongbox from under the bed, where she kept it. I set it on the dresser, and Mrs. Worth,

THE SECRET OF THE SEALED ROOM

fishing the key from beneath her nightgown (for she hung the key on a leather thong she wore around her neck), told me to get out.

She locked the door behind me, and I supposed she intended to count her money. She never did that where I could see. I had no idea how rich she might be, for she lived grudgingly, like a miser, never spending one penny more than she had to. Still, the strongbox was heavy, and the gold, silver, and copper money inside it clinked when it was moved.

Night came on, and after making sure the house was locked for the evening, I took a candle—not a clear-burning beeswax taper like the one Mrs. Worth reserved for herself, but a little mottled-yellow tallow dip, guttering in its own sooty smoke and giving a weak, reddish light—and climbed up to my small, windowless room. It lay on the top story, under the eaves, and its ceiling was unfinished, just rough splintery planking and beams. Worse, it slanted because of the pitch of the roof, so that even at the doorway I had to stoop to avoid bashing my head against a rafter.

My bed was only a thin pallet of folded quilts on the floor against the far wall, where the ceiling came down to within just three feet of the floor, and where the bell hung that Mrs. Worth would ring every morning to summon me. My pillow was not as nice as Mrs. Worth's goose-down ones, for it was stuffed with rags. Though it was almost the only home I could remember, I cannot say I liked the room. When he first bound me for seven years' service to Mrs. Worth, my father had told me with false cheerfulness that my little cuddy was better and more spacious than many a berth he had known at sea and had assured me that I had "room to swing a cat in," although what use that would have been to me or the cat the Lord only knows.

At any rate I soon fell asleep, though honestly I believe that I passed a full half of the night drifting on the very edge of waking, for I expected the bell to ring and summon me to my mistress's side. However, it remained silent, and sometime late in the dark hours I sank deeply into sleep and dreamed that my mother was alive again and that she offered me words of comfort, wisdom, and hope.

I woke with the musty scent of dust in my nose—for my little attic room was always terribly dusty, no matter how much I tried to scour it—and in my head the confused sense that something felt very wrong. As quickly as I could, I rose and dressed. As soon as I stepped into the hallway, where there were two windows, I saw that the day was far advanced. Sunlight poured in, the sunlight of nine o'clock at least, and that was very late indeed.

I tiptoed downstairs, thinking that Mrs. Worth must be making up for lack of sleep. The parlor clock showed me that it was nearly twenty past nine. Very quickly I set about my morning tasks, going out and feeding the demanding chickens, collecting eggs, and starting the kitchen fire. Our woodpile was dwindling, and soon enough, I saw, Mrs. Worth would have to order more. She was sure to complain about the cost, though Mr. Richard assured her that the man from whom he bought her wood was very reasonable in his rates, for he was somebody's slave who was now and then allowed to make a little money by cutting and selling firewood. Had he been a free man, Mr. Richard always vowed to Mrs. Worth, his prices would be twice as high.

Thinking that Mrs. Worth might relish griddle cakes for her breakfast, I mixed a batter and got everything ready. By then it was close to ten. Beginning to wonder and, truthfully, to worry, I went upstairs and tapped at Mrs. Worth's door. "Ma'am? I'm ready to cook your breakfast. Will you get up? It's late."

When she did not answer, I knocked again, louder, and called more loudly too. She did not respond. On the third try I pounded the door hard, thinking, *She will slap me for doing this.* When she still did not answer me, my heart began to beat faster in alarm. I tried the door and found that it was still locked from the inside. I did not spend much time wondering what to do, but rushed down the stairs and over to Mr. Richard's house. Betty Thayer let me in, and I sped past her exclamations of surprise and rushed into the parlor, where Mr. David sat slouched in a chair, his feet propped on a stool, reading a book. He glanced up, looking startled. "Why, Patience Martin! What is amiss, girl? You look—"

"Oh, Mr. David," I said all in a rush, "Mrs. Worth won't wake up, and her door is locked. I'm afraid she's very ill."

"Come," he said, springing up.

We ran back to the house and up the stairs. Mr. David pounded on the door so hard that the walls shook, but he was no more able to wake Mrs. Worth than I had been. He rattled the door in frustration. "Where is the key?" he asked me.

"She keeps it, sir. Last night she was counting her money—"

He stooped and put his eye to the keyhole. "The key is in the lock. Let's see if there is any other way in."

I could have told him there was not, but since he had taken charge, I followed him downstairs and out into the yard. The house was high and narrow, and though the bedroom had two windows that looked out on the far side toward the mainland, there was no way to climb up to them.

"We need a ladder," he said. "I know where I can borrow one long enough to reach. I'll need help, though."

He led me down Orange Street toward town. Along the way we met a tallish, strongly built boy who looked about my age. He was selling newspapers, and Mr. David clapped him on the shoulder. "Come with me. I have an errand to do, and if you help, I will pay you a shilling."

"Yes, sir," the boy said. "Newspaper, sir? Threepence."

He must have been selling early, for he had only three or four papers left, and Mr. David absently tossed him three copper pennies for one of them. As the paper changed hands, I saw that it was the *New-England Courant*. I had never read one because Mrs. Worth said it was a paper crammed with false and radical ideas and that it printed lies about the Reverend Cotton Mather, a man whom she thought not much inferior to an angel. We came to a carpentry shop, and Mr. David ran in for a few minutes. The boy stopped passersby and before long had sold the remainder of his papers. "A good day's work already done," he said in a self-satisfied way. He wore ink-smudged clothes, but he had a cheerful, ready smile. "Do you belong to that man?"

"No," I said.

"Whose slave are you, then?" he asked with a superior sort of glance.

My eyes flashed. "I am not a slave!"

He looked startled. "You aren't? From your coloring I thought you were a s—"

I saw the hateful word "slave" forming on his lips and snarled so formidably that he changed it in mid-speech: "—Spaniard!"

Despite my irritation his quick-wittedness tricked me into an unwilling smile. I turned my head away so he would not see it. "I'm bound as a servant," I told him. "That's all. My name is Patience Martin."

"So am I," he said in a strangely subdued voice. "To my own brother, until I'm twenty-one. An eternity! My name is Ben—"

"Come, boy!" It was Mr. David. Two men had hauled out a heavy wooden ladder. Mr. David hoisted the far end on his shoulder, and he motioned for Ben to pick up the trailing end. As Ben hefted his share of the ladder's weight, I noticed how broad his shoulders were. He seemed strong for his age. Mr. David looked back and called, "Ready? Don't stumble!" Between them they carried their burden back toward the house at a shambling pace. It looked heavy, and I was glad that Mr. David had found someone else to help with the weight. I did not think that I could have carried it the way Ben did.

At our house they set the ladder against the wall, though to make it reach the high windowsill they had to hold it at a steep angle, almost straight up and down. "I'm too heavy to go up with you bracing this," Mr. David said to Ben. "I'll keep the ladder from slipping. Climb up, will you, boy, and see if you can open the window and get inside. We believe my aunt is too sick to get out of bed, and her door is locked. The key is in the keyhole. "

"Yes, sir," Ben said. He scrambled rapidly up, like a sailor climbing the rigging of a ship. I had to swallow hard, for heights bother me, and I could imagine him pitching off the ladder and tumbling down on his head. However, he got to the window and called down, "The curtains are drawn, and I can't see anything."

"Try the sash!"

Ben pushed and rattled, and finally he was able to pry the sash open far enough to worm his way inside. "Unlock the door!" Mr. David called with his hand beside his mouth. "We're coming!"

Leaving the ladder in place, we rushed back up the stairs just as Ben turned the key and pushed the door open. His face was ashen. "Oh, sir—," he began.

Mr. David pushed past him, and I was not far behind. I smelled the reek of sour vomit as soon as I stepped into the dark room. I ran and opened the curtains wide to let daylight in. I turned as Mr. David stooped over the bed. "Patience," he said in a shaky voice, "run to my father's office and fetch him here. Tell him my aunt is dead."

Three

When death puts out our flame, the snuff
will tell if we were wax or tallow, by the smell.
—*Poor Richard's Almanac*

"Don't cry, Patience," Ben pleaded as we walked fast through the morning streets. Tears crept down across my cheeks, first warm and then cooling in the September breeze as we hurried along.

"Oh, hush!" My voice was little more than a snuffle, for I couldn't help crying a little. True, Mrs. Worth had never been kind to me, and Lord knew I had small reason to mourn for her, but she had given me a roof over my head and food to eat, and the thought of her dying with her unborn babe was so melancholy that I did weep a little for her.

"Well, you're only a girl, and girls love to weep, so—"

"Be still," I said furiously. "You know nothing about me! Why are you walking with me, anyway?"

"For company." He held up his hands as I glared at him and said, "All right, all right! It's something different, that's all. Anyway, if I go back to the shop, James will only find some task that doesn't even need doing and set me to it. Besides, I may be able to help you."

I turned my face away from him. "No one can help me."

"Still. You never can tell."

Since it looked as though I could not get rid of Ben without kicking him, I said no more and let him walk along beside me. Mr. Richard's office was all the way across town, near the Long Wharf. His business was shipping and trading, and he liked to be close to the harbor, where he could watch his vessels set out and return from voyaging. We arrived and stepped into the offices, a suite of dark little rooms that smelled strongly of tobacco. A clerk was perched on a high stool, working at a tall, narrow desk, its tilted writing surface no larger than a serving platter. The man glanced up as we came inside, his walnut-wrinkly face puckered in a frown. "What is this?"

"We've come with a message for Mr. Richard Worth," I said all in a rush. "We have news of his sister-in-law."

"Captain Worth's wife? The late Captain Worth?" The man hopped down from his stool and pulled at his badly shaven chin with ink-stained fingers. "I'll tell him you are here."

He went back into an inner room, and an instant later Mr. Richard bustled out. "What is it, girl?"

I told him that his sister-in-law lay dead, and that Mr. David was with her body. For a moment he only blinked at us. "Dead? Abedela dead? Are you sure?" he demanded.

"Yes, sir," Ben said. "I found her. She is dead."

"Who are you?" he asked.

"Benjamin Franklin, sir, apprentice to—"

Mr. Richard waved his hand. "It doesn't matter. I'll go there at once. Girl, do you know where Dr. Blackthorn's home is?"

"No—"

"I do, sir," said Ben. "I know it right well!"

Mr. Richard had seized a long coat that hung on a hook in the wall, though really the day was not very cool. The clerk helped to twitch him into it. Mr. Richard said, "Fetch the doctor, quickly. If that witch has caused my sister-in-law's death—what are you standing about for, you two? Go, tell the doctor to get to my brother's house as quickly as he can!"

I left with Ben, this time letting him lead the way. He threaded through narrow alleys and ducked down passages until we reached a good but not a rich house. Ben went to the back door and knocked, and when a servant answered, he said breathlessly, "Mr. Richard Worth has sent us with an urgent message for the doctor!"

The servant had us wait and went inside. In a moment the doctor himself came to the door. He was a tall, stout, square-jawed man of fifty or thereabouts, red-faced, gray-haired, and looking as if nothing could startle him. Again I blurted out the story and Mr. Richard's request that the doctor cut along to the Worth house as soon as he could. "I can go this instant," he said. "Half a minute."

He went back inside his house, and in the promised half minute, not a tick later, he stepped out again, wearing a decent long black coat, a bobbed white wig, and a black cocked hat. He carried a rattling leather bag, stuffed, I supposed, with physic and with instruments. Dr. Blackthorn mounted a sturdy gray mare and clattered away, leaving Ben and me to walk. "I will have to get back to the printing shop," he told me. "I hope I helped you some."

"Yes, you did," I said grudgingly, for he had made me angry with his talk of slavery and of weepy girls. "Thank you."

He gave me a shy kind of smile. "You're welcome."

Our way lay in the same direction for a while, and when we came to the street that led to his brother's printing shop, Ben pointed it out to me. "If you need my help again, that's where you may find me," he said. He rubbed his shoulders ruefully. "I may be a little lame if James is displeased, though. Sometimes he takes a rod to me if he thinks I am not doing my job well."

I nodded but did not reply, and we parted ways. When I got back to the house, I saw Dr. Blackthorn's gray mare tied to the hitching post out front. I went around to the back door and so into the kitchen. I could hear faint creaks from upstairs as the men strode to and fro in the bedroom overhead.

Despite everything that had happened, I felt hungry. Reasoning that the food in the house would surely go to waste, I threw out the griddle-cake batter I had made, which had thickened almost to a solid, and instead cooked eggs for myself, with a hot cup of tea. I even put a small chunk of brown sugar—a real luxury, because Mrs. Worth thought that sugar spoiled me—in the cup. The two eggs, a slice of bread spread with sweet butter, and the tea were the most delicious food I had tasted in days.

I finished my breakfast, washed the dishes, and then began to dust and sweep. Mostly, I believe, I was trying to busy myself so I would have no time to consider my situation. With my mistress dead, what would become of me? I thought that Mr. Richard might take me on as a servant, and that frightened me. His sister-in-law had a bad temper and was quick to strike out, but he was the sharper-tongued of the two and was even more convinced that girls were wholly evil. His cook, Betty Thayer, cringed when he spoke to her, and I did not like the beaten-down, fearful expression that always came upon her face in his presence. Wherever I should fetch up at the end, I could only hope I would not have to depend upon the charity of the cold-hearted Mr. Richard.

I was cleaning in the parlor when I heard the men clumping down the stair. "Send for the undertaker," the doctor was advising in a low voice, "and for the constables. You might see whether Moses White is at home. He's a magistrate."

"But are you sure it was poison?" asked Mr. Richard, dreadful words that froze me in my tracks.

"It was arsenic," the doctor responded flatly. "A physician cannot mistake the symptoms."

"Who would poison my aunt?" asked Mr. David. They had paused, it seemed, in the hallway, at the foot of the stairs, and from where I stood in the parlor, I could hear every word that passed among them.

"That I cannot say," Dr. Blackthorn replied, "for it is not my concern. I can tell you only that she was indeed poisoned, that she died of the effects, and that arsenic was the agent. The rest is a matter for the legal authorities."

In a low voice Mr. Richard said, "That witch Moll Bacon gave her some confounded magic potion made up of herbs. Could that—"

"Moll Bacon is a midwife and a good one," cut in Dr. Blackthorn sternly. "Many a woman in Boston is alive thanks to her care and her skills. If I were treating a woman in child and having a difficult time of it, I would call in Moll before consulting any Harvard-bred physician. My advice to you is to be exceedingly slow to accuse her of murder, Mr. Worth."

"You have your opinions, sir," snorted Mr. Richard, "and I have mine. David, go and seek out Magistrate White. Tell him what has happened, and bring him back here, if he is willing to come. And please notify the Chandler brothers that we have a body to bury. Amos knows me well, and he will call upon the reverend and make the necessary arrangements."

"Shall I ride Hero, sir?" asked Mr. David.

His father sounded irritated: "Yes, yes, take the horse."

Mr. David strode out into the parlor and was nearly at the door before he noticed me standing there so quietly. I believe I startled him, for he gave a sudden twitch of his head and said loudly, "Patience Martin! I had forgotten you were even here!" He lowered his voice and said with evident concern, "Child, perhaps you had better go to our house. Tell Betty to put you up somewhere for the night."

"Why should I do that, sir?" I asked in surprise.

He blinked at me. His eyes were large and liquid, the lashes as long and curling as a girl's. "Why, aren't you frightened to stay here in this house where a woman has died?"

"No, sir," I told him honestly. Despite all the goblin tales that folks spun about spirits and night terrors, I had never seen one, nor did I think that the ghost of Mrs. Worth would harm me—no more than she had while a living woman, at any rate, and that I could easily stand. After all, as a ghost she would have no hard and bony hand with which to strike me. Mr. David shrugged and went outside, and when I turned, it was to find the doctor and Mr. Richard gazing steadily at me.

"Girl," Mr. Richard said in his unpleasant voice, "did my sister-in-law eat or drink anything yesterday apart from that ungodly concoction the midwife brought? Think, now, for it is important."

"Yes, sir," I told him. "In the late afternoon she had a little bread and milk."

Mr. Richard gave the doctor a quick sideways glance. "So! And where did the bread and milk come from?"

Dr. Blackthorn was looking at me so intently that he made me want to lower my gaze, but I resisted that impulse and said, "The bread Mrs. Worth baked herself, on Tuesday, before she felt so ill. I borrowed the milk from your cook, Betty, sir."

Mr. Richard's face flamed red in a fierce flash of anger that surprised me. "Don't you dare make game of me, you hussy!" he snarled. "And don't make up lies! Why would my cook give you poisoned milk?"

"It wasn't poisoned, sir," I told him.

"How do you know?" Dr. Blackthorn asked me softly.

"Why, because I drank half of it myself, with my supper, sir," I told him. "And I was not ill at all."

"That's a good point," the doctor told Mr. Richard.

But Mrs. Worth's brother-in-law was still glaring at me, as though I had done something very sinful. "Did she eat or drink nothing else at all? Think, now!"

"No, sir. She didn't have much appetite."

"The potion," he growled in a tone of nasty triumph. He said to me, "Some people are coming to take Mrs. Worth away for burial. Stay here and be what help you can. I will decide later what is to be done with you. Come, Doctor, let's step out into the front. I dislike the air in here. It is positively mephitic."

I did not know what that word meant, but I presumed it was something bad. I finished as many of my chores as I could without going upstairs, and then I sat in the back room and read a little in *The Pilgrim's Progress*. I did not much care for the book, but unlike the almanac and the Bible, at least this one had conversations and pictures. Before an hour was up, I heard more voices. A woman and a man came in, both of them wearing black mourning clothing and both of them very quiet. They were from the undertaker's.

The woman and I went upstairs and cleaned Mrs. Worth's body—she had vomited all over the bed in her last agony. We dressed her decently in a good nightgown and made sure her eyes and mouth were closed, and then the man came in with another gentleman and they put Mrs. Worth onto a sort of litter and carried her downstairs and out to the street, where a horse-drawn hearse waited and where some of the neighbors stood in a loose, solemn group, gawping and murmuring. I remained indoors. With a sigh I picked up the dirty sheets and covers, and then I went back to the bedroom with vinegar and a pail of water and scrubbed the floor next to the bed. The room still smelled bad, so I opened both windows, not wide, but just to let it air out.

It struck me that Mrs. Worth had almost never opened her windows. She held that night air was unhealthy, and that by day there was dust. Now she had gone where she no longer had to worry about such things, and I hoped she was happy, wherever her spirit had gone. I sniffled a little once again at the thought that not only she, but her unborn child, had passed away.

It was only Friday, not Monday, but even so I thought it best to wash as many of the bedclothes as I could. Laundry took up my time for the rest of that afternoon, first heating the water and bending over a scrub board, and then wringing the sheets and things out and carrying them to the washing line, where the wind and the sun would soon dry them. I was hanging them out when two men came to reclaim the borrowed ladder. Not long after that, Mr. White, the magistrate, arrived at the house, where he inspected the bedroom and asked me a few questions. He seemed an elderly, indifferently gentle, forgetful man, half distracted with other thoughts and concerns, but he was kind enough in his own odd way.

Before sunset, just after I had taken in the dry laundry from the line in the backyard, and before I could fold it and put it away, Betty Thayer, wearing her usual sad expression of concern, came over and told me I had to leave and come to their house. "You can sleep in the kitchen, dear," she told me. "It is warm there, and it will do until Mr. Richard has time to think about your situation."

"What about our house?" I asked.

"A constable is to sleep in the parlor tonight," she told me. "And the house is to be locked tight until—until the authorities learn what they can about poor Mrs. Worth and how she passed away—oh, dear."

I got my few clothes together and went next door, trying to comfort Betty, who had bunched her apron into her hands and pressed it against her mouth, and who was crying into it with more tears and hard-gulping sobs than I had shown for my dead mistress. As I say, I felt some pity and sorrow for her, but now that she was beyond pain and worry, I thought it not so bad for her.

However, I said nothing of this to Betty. Nearly everyone thought me a wicked girl already, and with no place else to lay my head and no friend in the world, I hardly wished to do anything that would make her, too, turn against me. I had no great desire to sleep in the Worths' kitchen, true, but that was better than any alternative I could think of.

Four

Those who are fear'd, are hated.
—*Poor Richard's Almanac*

"You're a good girl, Patience. You remind me somewhat of my own dear daughter, Eliza," Betty Thayer told me the next morning, for by the time she rose, I had already started the fire in Mr. Richard's kitchen stove and was brewing a pot of tea. I knew from the times he had come to our house that tea was his customary drink. Betty was so pleased to have me for company that she gave me a smile, though it was melancholy enough, a wistful, sad sort of smile.

As I had started to do the day before, we cooked griddle cakes for the Worths' breakfast. Betty made a great many more than any two men could eat, saying comfortably to me, "We have to eat too." She was a fine cook, and her cakes turned out golden-brown and rich. To go with the griddle cakes we fried some good pieces of ham and several large eggs. These, with freshly churned butter and a little slice of cheese, made an elegant breakfast, I thought, delicious and far heartier than any that Mrs. Worth had ever offered me. The only thing missing that I secretly yearned for was maple syrup, for that had to be reserved for the Worth men, it being rather expensive. So Betty and I made do with gooseberry jam spread on our griddle cakes, and I told myself that its sweet, tangy flavor was almost as good as syrup. As we ate, Betty told me wistfully that it had been more than half a year since she had seen her own daughter, who herself was a bond servant. "Mr. Richard found her a situation," she said. "And I suppose we must be grateful that she has a place to stay and honest work to do."

I did not think she looked grateful, though.

Soon after breakfast Mr. David left the house to go and visit some friends of his in Cambridge, across the river. Betty told me he was often gone, for he and his father, she said, did not always agree, and Mr. David found it convenient to avoid quarrels when he could. Along in the latter part of the forenoon a lawyer, Mr. Cannon, came to the house, and he and Mr. Richard huddled together in the study. By that time I was growing very anxious, wondering what was to become of me, and so—I will confess it—I managed to wait quietly in the hallway near the study door and listen to most of what the two men said.

Their conversation concerned itself with matters of inheritance. The question of the estate was all perfectly in order, Mr. Cannon said. Mrs. Worth had made no will and had no immediate family, and so the deeds, the money, and everything would pass to her brother-in-law, who was next of kin. It should take only a week or so, the lawyer thought, to settle everything.

Mr. Richard expressed his satisfaction with that, observing that the property had belonged to his brother, anyway, and not strictly speaking to his brother's wife. He said he would arrange to rent or to sell all the houses, and he would take on the chickens and add them to his own backyard flock. At that the lawyer coughed delicately and asked, "And the servant girl, Martin? Will you provide for her?"

You may be assured that my face flamed a hot red when I heard myself being placed on the same level as a flock of hens!

"I don't want her. I'll sell her indentures," Mr. Richard growled. "Why should I burden my house with someone else's brat? Surely I can find someone eager to buy the remainder of her service. I can't use her here, and she'd be but another mouth to feed. I'll offer the remaining term of her service and make it a bargain—say just a pound a year, four pounds in all, a mere pittance. No one wanting a cheap servant girl could resist that!"

The lawyer sounded concerned. "Sir, think before you act, I pray you. As you say, I'm sure that at that rate someone would take the girl off your hands. But take care, for surely you want to leave her in a good Christian situation, sir, and you should not place her where someone might take advantage of her youth and innocence—"

"Hogwash," said Mr. Richard. "Once she is out of my sight and off my hands, her station in life is her own concern and lookout, so let her sink or swim—it is all one to me. This is a hard world, sir, and she must take her chances in it."

I waited to hear no more but turned from the doorway and stalked off, both of my hands clenched into angry fists. I knew my father had never wanted me to be treated as a piece of merchandise to be bought and sold, and I remembered my mother's melancholy account of the sad life lived by slaves in the Carolina country. What filled me with fury was the knowledge of the pain that my situation would cause her, could she have known of it. The stone-hearted indifference of Mr. Richard decided me: I would not let such a man dictate my whole future. From that very moment I began to plan my escape.

It seems odd to say it now, but at the time, with so much going on, some things that I should have considered simply never occurred to me. Not once did Mr. Richard ever ask me about the strongbox that held all Mrs. Worth's savings, and not once did I think about mentioning it. I did not know then that on the day after her death Mr. David and Mr. Richard had searched high and low through the house without finding the box. How could I? They never confided in me, and I knew only that they were in bad temper, the father much worse than the son.

The next day was Sunday, and we all went to church, with me sitting in the back crammed onto a pew with other servants. The following day, Monday, we were all back again for Mrs. Worth's funeral, a sad and lonely business with but few mourners. I saw her buried in the churchyard, in a plot that had a marker with her husband's name on it (though of course his body had not been recovered when he drowned, and so he was not buried there) and that would soon have another stone with her own name and dates of birth and death carved in it. I never liked that churchyard: The gravestones jutted from the earth randomly like the teeth of a giant, some leaning crazily left or right, some broken short. Many had dreary carvings on them of hollow-eyed skulls, and the very grass struggled to grow among them, straggling and stringy and half yellow. As soon as I could, I stole away, only to be scolded by Mr. Richard a few minutes later when he and his son left the grave site to walk home. I kept my head down and did not speak back, for I did not want Mr. Richard to grow angry and sell me before I had found some refuge.

I had not been idle in the time between moving into Mr. Richard's house and the funeral, but had stealthily gathered all my belongings—just my clothing, my little Bible that my mother had given me, and some shell necklaces and trinkets that my father had brought me from the Indies—into a small bundle. When Mr. Richard and Mr. David went back to Mrs. Worth's house late that afternoon, I slipped out with my bundle, with no clear idea of where I was going, except that it had to be somewhere away from being sold to another master or mistress.

The one possible person in all of Boston who might help me was young Ben Franklin, a sturdy and hale lad, but from his thoughtless appearance not one, I should say, given much to thinking and planning. I did not like his mistaking me for a slave, and I did not think he would ever be my friend.

He would have to do, though. I found a safe place to hide my bundle and walked up and down Queen Street, near his brother's printing shop. The prison was in the same street, and its dark, forbidding, heavily timbered walls made me so nervous that I did not dare even look that way, but kept my eyes to the other side of the street. At last Ben came out of the shop and hurried past the school that was next door to it, headed somewhere on an errand, and I quickly caught up to him. "You said you would help me," I told him.

He gave me a questioning glance. "So I did. What help do you need, Patience?"

"I need a place to hide," I told him. "I'm running away from my indentures."

He whistled. "That's serious!" He stared hard at me. "Are you really running away from your service? You're just a girl and you may not have thought this through properly."

"I'm a girl, but I'm just as sick of my indentures as you are of yours! And I'm running away from a man who would sell me for pennies," I said bitterly, and quickly told him of all I had heard.

"Well, that is a hard fate. All right, then, I will help. Have you no idea of some place to hide, even for a day or two?" Ben asked me.

"I have thought of one place, though it may be dangerous." I told him about the unrented house that belonged to Mrs. Worth, the hovel in Tanner's Lane.

"Let's go look at it," Ben suggested. He knew the back

ways of Boston far better than I, and we hurried along from one sheltered place to the next, attracting no attention in the busy afternoon streets. When I said something about not wanting people to recognize me, Ben chuckled. "If you must hide," he said, "hide in a crowd! When you're alone, people notice you. If you follow a family of six closely enough, they never give you another thought. You're just another daughter in a numerous brood!"

Tanner's Lane was horrible. It was small, with several dark passages and alleys, and the house we were looking for stood in one of these. The tiny patch of grass in front of the place was badly overgrown. The house not only leaned against the back wall of a tannery, but was actually an outgrowth of the business, almost a lean-to, its walls gray and splintered. We edged around it (for another old and moldy building crowded it on the left) and saw there was at least a back door as well as a front. Ben tried that and found it unlocked. I was not surprised. Only a desperate thief would break into that dismal hut.

But the inside was not as bad as I might have feared. It smelled bad from the tannery next door, and it was drafty, but it seemed reasonably dry. It offered shelter, at least. "I think you can sleep here," Ben said. "If you are not afraid."

"I'm not afraid." I hugged myself, for the inside of the

house (there were only two rooms) felt so dank, and of course I would not dare to build a fire, because the smoke would draw attention. "I'm cold, though."

"I can bring you blankets," Ben said. "And some water and food. But you won't be able to remain here very long, you know. Richard Worth will sell the house, if only for kindling, and you'll be discovered."

"I don't think that will happen for a week or more," I replied. "Not from what I heard the lawyer say, anyhow. By that time I hope to have hit on some other place to go." I looked at Ben. "What would you do in my place? Where would you go?"

"New York," he said promptly. "It's not as big as Boston, but 'tis a busy place, with strangers abounding. I could find work there as a printer. Or if not New York, perhaps Philadelphia, where they say the government is less oppressive than here in Massachusetts." He shrugged. "They don't kill people for being witches in Pennsylvania!"

"Nor do they in Boston," I said.

"But they did, not so very long ago," Ben told me, holding up a finger as if he were teaching a lesson. "Just over in Salem Village, nineteen or twenty people were hanged as witches twenty-nine years ago. And there are those in Boston who would gladly hang more even today!"

I thought of sour old Mr. Richard, so quick to say that Moll Bacon was a witch, and could not help agreeing with Ben. "I have heard of the Salem Village trials, but don't believe in witches," I said.

"I don't either," Ben assured me. "Have you ever heard of Chief Justice Holt in England? No? Once an old woman was brought before him and charged with being a witch. 'Why?' he asked. 'What makes you think she is a witch?' And her accusers said, 'Because she rides upon a broomstick!' And Justice Holt glared at them and said, 'And what if she does? I know of no law against that!' and with that he set her free!" Ben laughed at the thought.

"I wish all men in Boston were as wise as your Justice Holt."

"That's true. Even the students at Harvard prattle about witches sometimes, and you'd think they'd be learned enough not to believe in such things." He glanced outside. "I'll go now and fetch you something to eat and something to keep you warm. The nights are getting very cool."

"Wait a moment and I'll tell you where I've hidden my belongings, that you might fetch them, too."

I explained where, and he nodded. "Anything else?"

After a moment's thought I said, "You might bring me something to read. It's dull having nothing to do."

Blinking stupidly, he said, "Why, can you read?"

"Certainly I can!" I snapped. "I read very well. Better than you, probably!"

"All right, all right, something to read," he said hastily, and then he left, promising to return within an hour. Lord, but that was a tedious time! There was nowhere to sit but on the dusty floor, and more than once I heard the scrabbling of a rat behind the wall. I am not fond of rats, but I reflected that they were unlikely to live in the hut, which had been empty for so long there was no food for them, but rather would infest the tannery, where they could gnaw on the hides and leather. By the time Ben returned, I was if not at home in the place at least less fearful than I had been.

He brought a big cloth bag and spilled its bounty out on the floor: the promised blankets and even a small, threadbare cushion that would serve as a pillow, a loaf of good bread, a bag of dried apples, another of raisins, a big chunk of cheese, a sausage, some dry, flat bread, a bottle of water, and . . . a newspaper and some books. "I don't know what you like to read," he said. "This is by old Reverend Mather—since we were speaking of witches—and though I don't believe a word of it, it tells the whole sorry tale of the trials at Salem Village."

It was a book called *The Wonders of the Invisible World*, and it had been much read, so the pages were a little tattered. He had another called *The Thrifty Goodwife*, which was a volume of advice on how to keep house for a husband. I don't know why he thought I would like that. The newspaper was the *Courant,* which his brother printed each Monday, and he pointed out a story that he said would interest me:

> A Boston woman found Dead
> Died, Mrs. Abedela Worth, in Boston, aged about 33. She was the Widow of Captain Jared Worth who Died himself this Past July when his Ship sank suddenly in a Tempest off the Coast of Cape-cod. Mrs. Worth had been Ill but seem'd some Better when she went to Bed on Thursday night in her own House off Orange Street near Boston-Neck. The next Morning, she failing to Answer when her Lock'd door was knocked upon, relatives found an Adventurous Boy to climb up to her Window, where he Discover'd the melancholy truth, that during the Night, the Dread Hand of Death had Touch'd her.

"I wrote that," Ben said proudly.

"'Adventurous Boy'? You called yourself that?"

He shrugged. "It was an adventure to me."

"Do you write many pieces for the paper?" I asked.

"I have written poems," he said eagerly. "One on the drowning of a lighthouse keeper, and one on the taking of Teach, the pirate—they called him Blackbeard, you know. We printed them and sold a lot of them in the street. Did you read them?"

"Not I."

"Oh." He seemed a little disappointed.

"But I'm sure they were fine poems," I hastened to add. "Now you had better get back to your work. Can you see me here tomorrow? I'd like to contrive some plan of getting away from Boston—if I can do that with no money and no prospects."

"I'll see you as soon as I can," Ben promised.

That afternoon I read much of Reverend Mather's witchcraft book, thinking that he was a gullible fellow when it came to belief in magic and witches. The stories were horrible, and I could not help sympathizing with the poor men and women who were accused of witchcraft, locked up, sometimes tortured, and eventually hanged for their imaginary crimes. It seemed to me that if people like

Mr. Richard had their way, such cruelty would still be going on in Massachusetts. As I bundled up against the cold and fell asleep that night, I tried to comfort myself by thinking that soon enough I would run clean away from Mr. Richard, from Boston, and everything.

Though I did not know it then, I was quite mistaken. Very soon things were going to become much worse. Before another day passed, another person's life would hang by a thread, and only Ben and I could offer her a slender hope of living through a great ordeal.

Five

To whom thy secret thou dost tell,
to him thy freedom thou dost sell.
—*Poor Richard's Almanac*

Odd though it seems even to me, that night, trying to rest in a strange place, lying on a hard, dusty floor in an evil-smelling room festooned with cobwebs, I slept as well as ever I had done in my life. As was my habit, though, I wakened early, before the sun was well up, and in the palest light of dawn I found that the pesty rats had come in stealthily during the night and had discovered the food. They must have invaded in some force, for the thieving vermin had made off with all the remnants of the bread, nearly half a loaf, and had stolen every bite of the cheese.

They had spared me a little food, although they had also gnawed into the bag of dried apples. I picked out all the ones the rats had not chewed, and so I made my breakfast of water, raisins, and what apples the rats had spared. *This will never do,* I thought. I would have to find another and better place to hide, one where I would be beyond the reach of the marauding rats and beyond the knowledge of Mr. Richard. If I could but get away from Boston—but without money, without friends, without any refuge, I didn't see any way to escape the city. I might as well have been yearning to journey to the moon.

As I sat on the floor pondering all this, and before I had finished the last swallow of my poor, scanty breakfast, someone tapped softly at the door, and I heard Ben's voice: "Are you there?"

Rising to my feet, I opened the door and saw that the early sky gloomed gray overhead. It was one of those early fall days that could not decide whether to shower down a steady rain or to fade away in fog. Ben pressed inside, wide-eyed. "Here's news," he said, his tone urgent. "Did you know that Mrs. Worth had been robbed?"

"Robbed?" I asked. "How? Of what?"

"Of a box full of money," Ben said. "An iron box—"

"Oh, nonsense," I told him, flatly. "No one could have stolen that! I know right well where it is—stuck beneath her bed, just where she always hid it after counting her money."

"Well, Mr. Richard Worth says that it has been stolen."

Ben reached inside his shirt and pulled out a single half sheet of foolscap paper, black with smears of ink and heavily written across. Ben held it up. "And he thinks you took it," he said with what seemed to me an apologetic glance.

"What!"

"Read this," Ben urged.

I grabbed the paper and unfolded it. Mr. Richard's handwriting looked angry, as though with a sharpened quill he had all but slashed the black ink into the paper:

REWARD

For the return of a Runaway Wench. The Bond-Servant Patience Martin, about fourteen Years of Age, hath run from her Master, who offers a Handsome Reward of Ten Pounds for her Return. She may have about her a Case or Box of Iron, about a Foot Square and Four Inches thick, Lock'd, but she hath not the Key that fits it. She is a Molattoe, a light tan in Colour of Skin, with Strait Black Hair, of Shoulder length, of a Pleasant but Obstinate Countenance. She is of Middle Height for her Years, and Slender. She was last seen dressed in Blue Callicko, with no Bonnet, but her Hair tye'd back with blue Ribands. She talks Very smooth, and Lyes with great Alacrity. Trust not what she says. Whosoever finds her, if He shall take her in Charge, and *most Particularly return her Together with the Iron Box unopen'd, and Notify Mr. James Franklin at his Printing-House in Queen Street, over against Mr. Sheaf's School, shall have the Reward for her Return. By her Master, Richard Worth, Esq.*

"Oh! The lying old devil!" I felt like ripping the paper to shreds. Ben actually shrank away from my angry words: "I never took that box! How could I? Mrs. Worth always hid it in her room, and she locked the door that night, and it was still locked until you came in and opened it! Never after that was I for one instant alone in the room. I could not have taken the money box, and he knows it. 'Obstinate countenance! Lies with great alacrity!' The old devil!"

Perhaps I was so furious that I frightened the printer's apprentice. Ben backed away from me fearfully, I thought, holding up his hands as if begging for a truce. "Patience, Patience, I believe you! I know that you didn't steal that box or anything else. Here, see—I'm trying to help." He took from inside his shirt another paper, this one neatly printed, and handed it to me.

I unfolded that one, and saw that it was the same advertisement, but set into type as a broadside or poster. "How does this help?" I asked.

"Don't just glance at it. Read it through," Ben urged, pointing with an ink-stained finger, his chest puffing out a little, as though he were about to perform some conjuring trick that he was proud of. "Here. Here and here."

I read the lines and had to chuckle, despite my fit of anger. In setting the type the rascally Ben had changed the words. Now the paper described me as

an African Girl of Jamaica, Coffee-Black in Colour of Skin, with Curl'd Black Hair, Very short, of a Scowling Frowning and Obstinate Countenance, speaks with the Accent of the Isle of Jamaica. She is of Tall Height for her Years, and Fattish. She was last seen dressed in Green Muslin, wearing a white Mob-Cap.

"He will read this and know you tricked him," I said.

Ben grinned impishly. "That's the advantage of being a printer's apprentice. I printed up one copy just as he wrote it, and that's the one I have just taken to him and which he approved. The other copies, the ones the boys James hired are scattering through the town, read like this one. Do you think that Mr. Worth, having read the proof copy of the broadside through, will bother to read it again if he should see one in the street? I doubt it!"

"What if he does? He will know you changed it!"

Ben shrugged. "I will say that I dropped the case and had to reset the type, and in doing so confused his original with another advertisement for a runaway. The one I copied the new description for came in a week ago. It's reasonable enough that I accidentally gazed at the wrong manuscript while setting type. My brother James has done that himself— far too often, for though it seems like boasting, of the two of us I am the better printer!"

"Well," I said, returning the paper, "at least you may have made me safe for the time. But I won't be able to stay here." I quickly told him about my rat troubles. "I'll have to find another place to sleep. And even with your clever description out, I fear to go about the streets of Boston. Unless—I wonder if I could disguise myself?"

"That would be the very thing," Ben said decisively. He looked at me as though I were a waxwork. "I'll bring you different clothes. One of my friends works in a shop where they sell used clothes, and there are always piles of them that no one attends to. If I find you a bonnet, could you tuck your hair under it? And maybe we could use soot to darken your eyebrows?"

"I could do that. But I have no money at all—"

"Tush, let me worry about that. I've found that it is surprisingly easy to scrounge necessities, if you are satisfied with just what you need and no more." Ben cleared his throat. In a lower, troubled tone, he went on: "There is more news, I am sorry to say. Moll Bacon has been arrested."

I felt as though someone had struck me on the head. "Arrested!"

Ben nodded, his expression grim. "Mr. Worth swore a warrant against her, and she's been taken up on a charge of poisoning Mrs. Worth."

I saw at once what Mr. Worth had in mind. "Is he still claiming that the medicine she had me brew—"

"Aye," said Ben, without allowing me to finish. "That's how it is. And you see the danger, don't you? If you brewed the mixture that Mrs. Worth swallowed, and if the magistrates believe that was poison, you might be arrested as an accomplice or helper to the murderer."

"But that's just stupid! What reason would I have?"

"They know you did not like being a bond servant. And there's the box of money. Mr. Worth thinks you and Moll Bacon may have conspired to take it."

"That's an evil lie!"

Ben nodded. "You and I know it is, but it looks bad for

Moll Bacon. Mr. Worth has both reputation and money, and he'll surely have her thrown into prison if he can manage." He looked away and added in a scornful voice, "Have her hanged, if he can persuade a jury to convict her."

"I won't let that happen," I said. "I can't let that happen, not to an innocent woman!"

"What can you do?" Ben asked me. "You can't even leave this house right now. How can you help Moll Bacon?"

I set my jaw. "I can find out who really poisoned Mrs. Worth," I said.

"You? A girl?" Ben looked astonished, not amused.

"Yes, me, a girl. And you, a—a boy who thinks he's clever!"

"Me?" Ben asked, sounding startled. "But I can do nothing—"

I faced him squarely. "Oh, yes, you can! I need ears and eyes and legs that can run about Boston," I told him. "I have no one to help me but you."

"But I don't like the task," he objected. "I'm always in trouble with James as it is, and if my brother thought I was helping an accused murderer, he'd—why, he'd murder *me*!"

"Don't be a coward," I told him. "Ben Franklin, I need help, and you're the help I need!"

"Oh . . . fiddlesticks!" Ben ran his hand through his

longish brown hair. "'Tis really a stroke of luck for someone that you're running away from your indentures," he said ruefully. "For any master with you as a servant would be like a mouse trying to own a pet cat!"

Ben at first insisted that I should leave that rat-infested hovel at once, but I pointed out that until I could somehow disguise myself, the hut was safer for me than the streets. "But with big rats all around—," Ben began, looking distressed.

"I am bigger than any rat," I told him decisively. "I am not afraid of a rat!"

"All right, all right," Ben said, shaking his head and grimacing. "You are the most peculiar girl I have ever met!"

I crossed my arms. "Why? Because I am not silly and simpering and weak? Benjamin Franklin, I was not brought up that way! My father always told me that if one is to get ahead in life, one must take fortune in hand and be independent!"

"That's a fine sentiment," Ben agreed. But then he added, "Provided one isn't a slave or a servant."

"I will not be a servant all my life." Nor any of my life from there on, I vowed silently. I thought again of Mr. Richard offering to sell me, or at least sell four precious years of my time on earth, at such a mean, low price just to get me off his hands. He would not have done such a thing to a cow, if Mrs. Worth had kept one! He would have had more consideration for a beast than for me.

"Hurry and bring me some clothes," I told him. "I don't want to spend another night here, not because of the rats, but because Mr. Richard might take it into his head to come round and inspect the houses he now owns."

"It will take some time," Ben warned. "My brother won't be happy that I've been so long on my errand as it is."

He left, and I waited. Outside, the fog lowered and lowered, until it rolled in the streets, turning the one window into a little gray pane of soft light. Directly beneath it I sat on the floor, and having nothing else to do, I fell again to reading in Cotton Mather's witchcraft book and snorting in disbelief at all the wild imaginings he put forth as sober truth. A man he called G. B., a minister, had provided followers of the Devil with poppets or dolls, and by sticking thorns in them, the witches had caused people to suffer bodily pains. And what, according to the author, were the sure proofs of this man's wickedness? How could the people of Salem Village have known that G. B. was truly a sorcerer in league with the Devil? Why, he picked a basket of strawberries faster than another man! He was strong, and he could pick up a keg that another man could not lift! These silly, trivial things were enough for Reverend Mather to claim that the man had surely sold himself to the Devil, and that he had then sent his familiar imps to torment honest, godly people. Was it true, I wondered, was it possible, that a minister like Cotton Mather thought that God was so puny and weak that such foolish things were even possible?

Then again, the book told of a poor woman named Elizabeth How who had been tried, found guilty, and hanged as a witch. The name was familiar, for I had heard Mrs. Worth telling tales to her neighbors about the same woman, whom her mother had known very well. And though Mrs. Worth spoke scornfully of her, two old women who had been acquainted with Mrs. How had told Mrs. Worth that the accused witch was a gentle soul and that she took tender care of her blind husband, who, had tried to defend her and had tearfully protested her innocence to the end. The Reverend Mather found her grievously evil:

> *It has been a most usual thing for the Bewitched*
> *persons, at the same time that the Spectres*
> *representing the Witches Troubled them, to be*
> *visited with Apparitions of Ghosts, pretending*
> *to have bin Murdered by the Witches then*
> *represented. And sometimes the confessions of*

the witches afterwards acknowledged those
very Murders, which these Apparitions charged
upon them; altho' they had never heard what
Informations had been given by the Sufferers.
There were such Apparitions of Ghosts testified
by some of the present Sufferers, and the Ghosts
affirmed that this How had Murdered them:
which things were Fear'd but not prov'd.

Ghosts and murders! Things feared but not proved! Though the Reverend Mather steadily tried to turn the reader's mind against Elizabeth How, I could not help thinking that hers was a case like mine. Like Elizabeth, I believed in standing on my own feet and did not gladly suffer fools. Like her, I was suspected of something—stealing Mrs. Worth's money box—that was "feared but not proved." And like her, I fretted, should I be taken, I would have no hope in a court of law, for Mr. Richard was as set against me as Reverend Mather had been against those poor women of Salem Village who were falsely accused of witchcraft.

It seemed incredible to me that men had ever believed in witches. I had even heard that some eight or ten years ago, the Great and General Court had ordered all the convictions of the "witches" to be reversed, and for the victims of the witch persecution all to be declared innocent. That was, I supposed, a good thing in its way and a victory for common sense over superstition. Yet what comfort could the court's words be to a score of innocents who had been put to shameful public deaths because of false charges? And though all people of sense had long ago admitted that what had happened in Salem Village in 1692 was mere bloody-minded foolishness and the malice of small minds, I knew that many in Boston still maintained that the accused had truly been witches. Indeed, on many an occasion I had heard Mrs. Worth gossip about magic and the Devil and evil sorcerers (she thought Indians especially were in league with Old Nick), and Mr. Richard had been mighty quick to call Moll Bacon a witch. I felt sorry for Moll, with such a persecutor as Mr. Richard against her, and though she would surely have her day in court, I wanted to take no chance with that kind of justice.

For long hours I chafed, until finally Ben returned in the afternoon, emerging from the dense fog with more food for me—some slices of roast beef tucked into a split roll, so I could eat it without fork or spoon—and a bottle of apple cider. I wolfed it down, I am afraid, for even though I had been sitting unusually idly for me, hunger had crept upon me. He also had brought a bundle of clothing: a very plain dark-gray, almost black, dress, and a black bonnet of a style I recognized at once. "Quaker clothing!" I said, surprised. In the last age Quakers had not been tolerated in Massachusetts, had even been put to death for their beliefs, though now they were numerous enough and were mostly ignored, as they largely kept to themselves.

"It's a good disguise," Ben insisted. "No one looks twice at a Quaker nowadays. And they're supposed to be humble and gentle, so you can keep your head down and hide your face inside the shade of the bonnet. If you think you can act humbly and gently."

I glared at him. "What is that supposed to mean!"

"I'm only saying I think it's a good disguise," Ben said, with a placating smile.

I took the clothing into the little hut's only other room and changed into it. Ben had a fair eye, I had to admit, for without him knowing what my body measured, the clothing fit me well enough, only a bit too broad in the shoulders, but that was hardly noticeable. And I could tuck my hair completely under the bonnet. "How do I look?" I asked him, coming back into the sleeping room.

"Good, good," Ben said, considering me from head to toe. "The black clothing makes you look a little paler. Let me do your eyebrows."

From the back of the cold stone fireplace in the other room he took smudges of soot, and with the tip of his little finger he brushed it onto my eyebrows, tilting his head and sticking out the pink tip of his tongue in concentration. "There," he said. "That will pass, if someone doesn't come within a foot or so of you and look closely. I've changed the shape a little. It makes you look different. Not so cross and scowling."

"I am not cross and scowling!"

"Well, it changes you, anyway," Ben said.

"But what am I to do for a place to stay?"

"I have that solved too," Ben told me. "James has complained that I leave the shop too cluttered and too untidy, and I always protest that I have not the time to clean it. We will go to him and I will say that you are from a large family—he will believe that; our own family is enormous—and that your parents, being poor, want you to find a respectable way to earn your bread. You will offer to work for your meals and a few pennies a week, and James will hire you—I know he will, for he will see that as a bargain—and the best part is, there is a kind of large cupboard or closet in the shop, unused and empty, where you can sleep at night, and he will be none the wiser!"

"That seems a risk to me," I said.

"Come, girl," Ben urged. "You say you want to free Moll Bacon from suspicion! What better place to be than the newspaper, where word of everything that happens in town is sure to come? We will work together—you will tell me what to do, and I will be your eyes and ears and legs about town, just as you said. We'll free Moll from all charges of poisoning and murder, and we'll prove that you did not run away with the box of money, and I know that with that question answered, Mr. Richard will bother no more about you. Do you think he wants you? No, he wants the money!"

Ben had a good point; I could not deny that. Nor could I think of a better plan. And so, that very afternoon, in the guise of a plain, humble Quaker girl seeking some honest employment, I went with Ben through the heavy fog to Queen Street, where his brother James ran his shop and printed the *New-England Courant*. It occurred to me fleetingly that in a way this was a test. If I did not want to be a servant—and Lord knows I did not!—then if I could secure and hold a job with Mr. James Franklin, why, I could make my own way in the world.

And if into the bargain I could save an innocent woman's freedom and perhaps her very life, so much the better.

Six

Write things worth reading, or do things worth writing.
—Poor Richard's Almanac

As Ben suggested, I asked his older brother James for employment timidly, in my quietest voice, my eyes on the floor and my whole demeanor humble. James, who was an older and heavier edition of Ben, asked what wages I would take, and when I named a very low payment indeed, he immediately told me to pick up all the scattered papers that covered the floor—carefully, for I had to stack them neatly in a scrap-paper bin, separating those that had a blank side from those already printed over—and then to find the broom and sweep.

And so that very afternoon, a quiet one with the heavy fog muffling the sounds of passing horses and footsteps out in the street, I worked for wages for the first time in my life. It was hard enough toil at first, the dear Lord knows, for honestly, I don't believe that either James or Benjamin Franklin had set hand on a broom for the whole time the shop had been there. Indeed I was surprised to find that the shop even possessed a broom, since it seemed untouched by one! Sweeping up was a dusty, nose-tickling, difficult task. And once I had swept the whole place out, there were scores of smaller matters to attend to: trimming the candles so they burned clear, filling three lanterns with oil, cleaning the dirty, mud-spattered windows, and on and on, always something to keep me busy.

As I worked about the shop, I quickly learned that James Franklin had a wide circle of acquaintances, and indeed many of them were young men who loitered away the afternoon in the printing house, cracking jests and proposing scandalous articles for the *Courant* that, had Mr. James actually printed them, would have quickly landed him in prison for treason or worse. There were never fewer than two of them lazing away, gossiping and joking and distracting Mr. James from his business—but not Ben, I noted, for he, like me, always had his hands full.

All the while, the press ran, for printing the newspaper was about the least of the concerns in that place, where anyone with the silver could walk in and ask for this or that to be set in type and run off. Perhaps Mr. James was simply popular, but he had a steady stream of customers with little jobs for the shop. There were broadsides to be printed, like the one that gave such a poor description of me, and broadsides of ballads, and legal forms, and I don't know what else besides, but almost constantly Ben or one of the other young men who worked for Mr. James was either setting type or else pulling the big lever of the press, and someone else was putting in fresh sheets of paper or taking out the finished, printed copies.

Even after I had spent hours cleaning up, the whole place reeked of ink, though as I had gotten used to the far more unpleasant stench of the tannery, I supposed that soon enough the sharp smells would cease to offend my nose. Everything in the print room, every visible surface, was smudged and smeared with ink too, and had I been a thousand cleaning girls, each one wielding a scrubbing brush and armed with soap and a bucket of hot water, I should never have been able to remove all the splotches had I worked for a hundred years.

It had grown quite late in the foggy afternoon, and the lanterns had all been lit, when a tall man of about thirty years' age came in and sank into a chair. "Here's someone who will bring us news," said James Franklin, and the two other young men who still lingered chatting fell silent. James sat down near the newcomer and asked, "What is disturbing Boston these days, Constable Wilkes?"

"Murder and thievery and conniving," said the man in a deep, rumbling voice, leaning back in his chair and yawning. "The same as ever, Printer Franklin. Human iniquity does not change, sir, nor in my opinion shall it alter before dooms-day comes."

"What news of the poisoning?" Ben asked from his place at the press, and you may be sure that I listened very closely indeed to hear the answer to that question.

"Oh, that. We have taken Moll Bacon in on charges, and she is lodged yonder in a tight-locked jail cell this very minute," Wilkes said, nodding toward the street and the nearby prison house. "We are inquiring diligently about the poisoning. Men have turned the Bacon woman's house topsy-turvy a-searching for her poisonous brews."

"And found none?" asked Ben.

"None that I've heard of," admitted Wilkes. "But that proves nothing, of course, except that she may have been so cunning as to hide her stores of the villainous stuff somewhere else. Let's see, what other news . . . oh, I know that you've heard of the runaway servant who may have been the Bacon woman's accomplice, because I saw the broadsides you printed."

Mr. James nodded. "Yes, the Martin girl. We did that job for Richard Worth, and he was so eager for it that he put good silver money in my hand—a rare thing for him, who usually must be billed and then dunned for weeks until he pays the bill. Prudence Martin. No, wait, Patience was her name. Has she been found?"

"No, not yet, but she soon will be," Wilkes assured him with a superior, knowing air. "A runaway boy can sometimes show us a clean pair of heels and get away, but for a wench the business of escape is much more difficult, and in the end they always turn themselves in if we don't catch them. We shall have this Patience Martin before long, never fear."

"Girl," James said to me, pointing to a shelf behind me, "fetch that lantern closer. It's almighty dark this afternoon, with the fog."

"Yes, sir," I whispered, and I took the lantern over and set it on a round table beside Constable Wilkes's chair. He was busy blowing his nose, great bubbling honks in a big white linen handkerchief, and I do not know if he even looked at me when I came so close. Had he wanted, he could at that moment have laid hold on the Martin girl by merely stretching out his hand.

"New cleaning girl?" Wilkes asked, his voice strangely

pinched as he wiped his nose with the handkerchief, which looked to have had several days' use already.

"Yes, sir," I said, my eyes modestly lowered. "Just hired today, sir."

Constable Wilkes chuckled and darted a teasing glance at Mr. Franklin. "That's very well for this hog-wallow! 'Tis high time James employed someone to keep this disgrace of a business in some order," he said. "What is your name, girl?"

"Mercy," I said, not looking up, and giving him the same false name I had given to James Franklin earlier. "Mercy Dyer."

Wilkes nodded, putting away his fouled handkerchief. "Yes, I know some Quaker Dyers," Wilkes agreed. "Are you related to—"

Ben, who had just finished his printing job, came to my rescue, sliding up to Mr. Wilkes's elbow with a quick interruption: "About the Worth woman and the poisoning, Mr. Wilkes—has the money been found, sir? The money missing from Mrs. Worth's house, I mean?"

I quickly made my retreat to the back of the shop, as the constable, who seemed to have a deep love of gossip, turned to face Ben and replied: "As to that, why, we're not absolutely sure that it is money at all—just an iron box, which must be very heavy for a girl to lug around." He scratched his nose and said, "You were the boy who climbed in through the woman's window, were you not?"

"Yes, sir."

"Did you notice anything amiss? Anything strange?"

Ben shrugged. "Well, the woman lay dead. That and the smell—a terrible smell of vomit and of garlic."

"Yes, the garlic smell is what made the doctor call it arsenic poisoning. The key was in the lock?"

"It was, sir. I turned it and let Mr. David Worth in."

"Aye, and we know the story from that time forward. What did you ask about? Oh, yes, the missing strongbox. For all we know, I was saying, it might contain anything! But the great probability is that it does hold money, possibly a tidy sum, too, since Mrs. Worth collected rents and interest on her husband's investments, and none of that has turned up in her house. I'd wager that if it *is* the widow's fortune, the runaway servant girl has been disappointed in stealing it, for Richard Worth has told us that the box had a very secure, heavy lock, and that they found the only key hanging on a cord around the dead woman's neck."

"Perhaps she could smash the lock," Ben suggested.

Wilkes flapped his hand. "A weak girl could never hope to break into so sturdy a box, my boy. You, now—I've heard what a conniving rascal you are, sir, and I'm sure you think breaking into such a strongbox is easy, but a girl is different entirely. 'Twas foolish of the wench to steal only the box and not the key as well, but there you are! Girls are not very strong, and they are certainly not very bright."

That led James to a tedious long jest about a foolish woman and her cow, and Wilkes countered with one of his own, and then another of the young loiterers was reminded of yet another, and between the four of them they told so many stories of foolish females—none of them funny to me, to be sure—that I took my leave of the print shop while they were still talking. Ben had arranged things with me, and I simply walked around to the back of the shop, where a rear door led into a storage room heaped with paper, ink, lamp oil, and other stuff. The door was closed, of course, and locked from the inside, so I simply stood there, huddled in the fog, and waited.

A moment later Ben opened the door and let me in. From the front of the shop I could hear the laughter of Mr. James, Mr. Wilkes, and the other two young men, still cackling over the supposed witlessness of women. "In here," Ben whispered, opening a low hatch of a door, probably no more than four feet tall, as it led into a low kind of space, which—to my pleasure—I saw had been swept quite clean. At least Ben had thought of that!

He had called the space a closet, but it really was more like a tiny little room, about seven feet long, five feet high, and four wide. Very likely it had been built to hold firewood when the building was put up and the back room had been a kitchen, but now the only stove stood in the main office, where it would give heat in the winter, and beside it there was a big, splintered wooden crate that held the fuel.

"Will this do?" Ben asked me in a hushed voice.

"Very well," I told him in a whisper. It was far cleaner than the decaying old hut in Tanner's Lane, and much less drafty.

Ben sighed his relief at finding that I had no objection to the place where he proposed to stow me. He had placed my rolled-up bedding in there already and had left me a candle. "I will not turn the key in the back door lock—the door is just bolted, which will do well enough. If you hear footsteps coming," Ben whispered, "blow out the candle and keep very still. James has never even opened the closet door to my knowledge, but if he sees light coming through the cracks—well, he shall be gone in a few minutes, and I with him, and as always I will lock the print shop behind us. I'm sure you'll be safe for the night. You have some water there in that bottle, just behind your blankets, and I've put in a little more food. There is"—he turned very pink—"I mean, if during the night you have—a sudden need—"

I understood what he was too embarrassed to say. "I know there is a privy not ten steps from the back door. If I have to go to the necessary house in the night, I will be sure to bolt the back door again when I return."

"Oh," Ben said, not even able to look me in the face.

"Girls have to go to the toilet now and then, just as boys do," I said, enjoying his squirming.

He nodded and muttered, "Uh—good. Well—good night!"

"And good night to you."

As Ben had expected, the sounds coming from the shop fell off, and before long everything had grown quite silent. I had my supper: cheese and bread and a couple of pears. Afterward, peeking out, I found that night had fallen. I got ready for bed. Ben had promised to come in early enough to waken me and let me dress so I could leave the shop from the back, coming back to the front to be admitted for my day of work—"James has me open up," he had explained, "for he likes to rise late and linger at the breakfast table of a morning, but I think a man who goes to bed early and rises early has a better chance in this world, so I never mind coming ahead to unlock the shop."

I did light the candle after I was sure everyone had gone. An advantage to being here and not home or in the hut in Tanner's Lane was that I found much to read, for James kept a shelf of books in the back storage room of the shop. Many of them were hardly worth my attention, being collections of sermons, or mathematical treatises, or dry instructional volumes on how to build things, or agricultural tomes on how to grow things, or dull academical works that tried to explain the nature of things.

Among all these he had a few storybooks, though, and that night, by the smoky orange light of a cheap, dripping tallow candle, I began to read a newish English book that told about the adventures of a man named Robinson Crusoe. It had the earmarks of an imagined tale, with much exaggeration, and I did not think for a minute that any of it was true, but in a way I felt akin to poor Robinson, who came to be cast away on a desert island, alone and without friends.

The little closet was in its own way my island. But then at least I was not all alone. I had Ben. Although he had pigheaded ideas about girls, he at least was willing to help me.

The next morning when Ben tapped on the door of my sleeping compartment, he looked utterly surprised when I opened it and ducked out, already quite awake and fully dressed. "I expected you would still be sleeping," he said. "Sunrise is half an hour off!"

"It is as you said," I told him. "If I'm to stay free and uncaught, I must be sharp, and that means I must be early to bed and early to rise as well."

"Yes," he agreed, chuckling. "I see you are much of my mind!" He was holding a candle in a pewter candlestick and handed it to me as he reached down to the floor for a little bundle. "Whatever the constable's opinions of female intellects, you are a wise girl, Patience. Here, I have brought us more food for breakfast. This is porridge seethed in milk—I cooked it myself, for my mother has all my brothers and sisters to cook for, and I don't like to make her get up before dawn. It's still warm, because we don't live far from here. And here is a real treat—an orange!"

"I have never eaten one," I told him, gazing at the large fruit he held out. It seemed to glow.

He dragged in two of the chairs that Mr. James's friends had been sitting on the previous afternoon, and we had quite a nice breakfast there in the storage room, using a third, broken chair as a kind of low table between us. Ben had brought a little covered cast-iron pot with the hot cooked oats inside, and two wooden spoons. We ate from the pot, taking turns.

It was delicious, for he had dripped some molasses in to sweeten the porridge. Then he peeled the orange—I had never smelled anything so heavenly—and I saw that it came apart in juicy little crescent-moon sections. We ate these, dividing the orange between us, and I was amazed at the taste, tart and sweet at the same time. It was glorious.

Ben saw that it pleased me, and he said, "It seems to me that somehow, I know not how, this fruit soaks up the sun itself and then gives it back to us in juice and pleasant flesh. 'Tis a pity that they are so dear in expense. I know nothing like an orange to bring a cheerful hint of sun to the cloudiest, saddest day."

He quickly tidied up after our meal—he could be a neat boy when he stirred himself, I saw—and told me never to worry about being caught. "I hope you weren't too oppressed by loneliness," he said.

"Not at all. I was reading a—oh! I almost forgot to put it back!" I fetched *Robinson Crusoe* from the closet.

"I love to read," he said, nodding at the book I was replacing in the shelf. "At night when I can, I take a book home, or if James forbids that, I come in early, with my breakfast, and read for an hour or so before I have to start work."

"I love reading too," I told him. "Though I've had little chance to do it up to this time of my life."

"Tell me about your life," Ben asked, leaning forward in his chair, knees on elbows, chin in hand.

"There is not much to tell," I responded with a rueful smile, sitting back in the chair. I felt a little flutter of pleasure. It was such a luxury to sit and just talk! "And anyway, did you not hear Mr. James and his friends? Women are foolish, flighty creatures, and their thoughts and opinions are of no value!"

"I am not James," Ben said. He smiled too, and in that moment I had the curious feeling that he was younger than I, though in truth he was a year or more older. "I'd like to hear about your life, and I don't mind telling you about mine. I will start. There were ten children in my family, to begin with, but one of us died."

He went on, telling me of his hopes and his failings and his ambitions. He was often in his father's bad graces, for, as he admitted, he had too ready a tongue. "For instance," he said, shaking his head, "my father says the longest graces over meals! Prayers that go on until the rest of us are perishing of mere hunger. So once, when I was about eight, when he was putting up a great barrel of salted beef for our winter's meals, I had a wonderful idea. I said, 'Father, why don't you say one long grace right now over the meat, once and for all? 'Twould be a great saving of time later on!'" He laughed, but rather sadly. "Father did not think that very funny or very wise, either. Lord, what a tongue-lashing I received for being blasphemous and ungodly!"

He spoke of other things, of how he had attended the Latin School in town for two years. It was a happy time, but then his father decided that Ben was such a disobedient boy that he had no likelihood of being called to the ministry and would not need such an expensive education. Ben had to be content with another year or so of cheaper common schooling. "And then there was the question of what was to become of me," he said. He told me that he longed to run away to sea, but that an older brother of his had done just that and now his father and mother treated the boy as dead to them. For a while he had been apprenticed to a candle maker—"Dull, greasy, awful work," he said, making a face. "I would hate to spend my life as a tallow-chandler." His father at last agreed to let Ben change, so now he was on his way to becoming a printer.

After he had been so open with me, I could not very well refuse to tell him anything. I spoke of how my father had stolen my mother away from her owner in Charleston, and how he had married her and had brought her to Boston to live a free life. Ben knew already of how my father had died, in the wreck of Mr. Jared Worth's trading brig the *Swiftsure*, along with all the other men aboard her that terrible, storm-torn July day, eighteen more souls in all. I even spoke of my mother and how she had died of smallpox when I was only ten.

Ben nodded gravely and said, "Smallpox is a terrible scourge. Back in June it seemed that every other house had a quarantine sign tacked on the door, and Lord knows how many died. I suppose your mother died in the last great epidemic before this present one."

"Yes," I said. I really did not want to speak of my mother and of how I had lost her.

"They inoculate for smallpox now," Ben said. He grimaced. "Although James is against the whole idea. That is what got him in hot water with Reverend Mather—Reverend Mather thinks everyone should be inoculated against the disease, and James printed that this was mere delusion and superstition and tempting God, to open a vein and put the smallpox in!"

"I believe it works," I said. "My father took me to Dr. Zabdiel Boylston, in Brookline, and father and I were both inoculated in June, just before Father left on his last voyage. It didn't hurt much, and I hardly got sick at all."

"Oh, it was not a question of truth so much," Ben said, shrugging. "It was just a way for James to get at Reverend

Mather, for he despises the way the old Puritans still try to rule over Boston. There are a great many of them, you know, some powerful, and though you and I may not believe in witches, they still do. That's why we have to be careful in trying to help your friend Moll Bacon—"

We heard the front door of the shop open, and Ben skipped up, closing the closet door and silently opening the back door of the shop. I slipped out quickly and quietly, waited in the cool dark morning for a few moments so my heart would not be pounding quite so hard, and then went around to the front of the shop and came in as Ben was replacing the chairs we had borrowed. Mr. James was lighting one candle from another and glanced over at me as I came in. "There you are, Mercy. You're a conscientious worker to come on time. It's turning chilly. Grab some of the scrap paper and some kindling and make a fire in the stove, there's a good girl, and then I'd like to have this inky, mud-caked floor really well scrubbed just for a change. As soon as the stove is going, put on some scouring water to heat. Ben, here's sixpence. Run and buy a mop and pail. Not an expensive one, mind, and if there's change—"

"I know," Ben said. "I'll bring it straight back to you."

And so my second day of working for wages began. The time I put in would have been dreary indeed had I been, as my friend Benjamin was, bound to service, with not even a few pennies promised as pay, but as it was, I did not feel so bad. Come the end of the week I would receive payment, however small, for my work, however hard, and that fact let me feel that I was behaving in a very grown-up fashion. Even that ill-burning stove could not fully take away my pleasure at what I was doing or the sense of responsibility I felt.

Still, all through that second busy day, I could not keep from worrying and wondering. How would I be able to help Moll Bacon? When would I have the time even to try?

And supposing I did try, could I do enough? Could I do anything at all? Ben tried to keep my spirits up, but I declare, that day I began to envy him. The weather had changed with the coming of day. It was sunny but much colder, and a blustery west wind huffed and whined and swept all the fog clean from the streets.

I could only view this through the window, but Ben was able to get out in the sunshine, for Mr. James kept sending him here and there on various errands, and though I believe he worked as hard at the press as I did with the mop, at least he got out and had some freedom to run through the streets of Boston. I had none of that. I truly believe that until all the trouble began, though I yearned for freedom, I did not fully understand just what it was, or how precious.

However, though I did not then know it, Ben felt the same constraint as I, and wanting to help me, he was already thinking up a plan to do something about Moll Bacon's problems.

As it turned out, it would be a dangerous plan for the both of us.

Seven

The Vicious choose the night season.
—*The Pennsylvania Gazette*

That afternoon Mr. James left the shop early, he having an obligation to dine with the parents of Ann White, a young lady he was courting, and I left as he did, but turning the opposite way. As soon as I knew he was out of sight, I quickly retraced my steps and returned to the shop, behaving as though I were upset about having forgotten something, and Ben, who had been left to close everything up and lock the doors, let me in.

We left the front of the shop dark, so that no one would try to come in and ask to have something printed, and we went to sit in the back, where we had breakfasted that morning. Ben then shut the door to the printing room so that we could have light. Once again Ben shared with me food that he had bought on his last errand. I remarked that he seemed to have money enough for one who was not being paid, and he shrugged and smiled. I suspected, but did not know for sure, that when he sold his newspapers on the streets he was taking a penny now and again. I said nothing about that to him, for if he was pocketing some money, he was doing it for me, and so I saw no way that I could make an objection and still get something to eat each day.

I told him that I would need another dress very soon, so that I could wash the gray one, and he promised to find more clothing for me. "It should be easy," he said. "There are a good many used clothes in my friend's father's shop, so many that they mend only the very best and sell the others by the pound, as mere rags. I'll warrant I can find another just as good as this one. I think black next time, to make thee a more proper Quaker lass."

"Behave with some respect, you knave," I told him, "or *thou* might find my hand boxing *thy* ears."

Ben laughed. "Stop it, stop it. Don't try to talk like an old-fashioned Quaker," he said. "Only the very old ones use 'thee' and 'thou' outside of their church nowadays! Just speak as thou normally do. *Dost*, I mean." He did not share my meal with me this time, but watched as I ate and asked, "Is the food good?"

It was, for he had found somewhere a nice slice of cold chicken pie, very tasty, and I told him as much. "But help me think now. We have to devise some way to help Moll," I told him.

Ben heaved a deep sigh. "I'm cleverer with things I can do with my hands than with my head. I just don't know what we can do. Can you think of anything?"

I pondered for a few minutes. "This occurs to me," I said between mouthfuls of the savory chicken pie. "We could have someone examine the little bag of herbs that Moll had me brew into a tea. They do think the tea was poisoned?"

"That's what everyone suspects," Ben admitted thoughtfully. "But no one has suggested that the bag of herbs ought to be found and studied. I don't think the authorities have it. Had the constables found it, surely Mr. Wilkes would have said something."

I wiped my mouth and took a long drink of water. "If Mr. Richard is so certain that it held poison, why does he not search for it?"

Ben scratched his head. "A good point, but does he even know about the tea? Did he see you brew it?"

Thinking back, I said, "No, he didn't see me. I was in the kitchen, and he was in the parlor. But I did tell him that I was to make the tea, and I showed him the pouch of herbs."

Ben frowned and tapped his toe impatiently on the floor. "What if Mr. Worth is himself the poisoner?" he asked slowly. "He is the one who will inherit houses and holdings, after all, so he would have reason to want Mrs. Worth out of the way. Perhaps he did not tell the constables about the herbs because he knows they contained no arsenic. He may even have destroyed the bag."

"I don't think he would even know where to look for it," I told Ben. "And I am sure that it was not poisoned. Could we prove Moll's innocence, do you think, if we could let someone examine the herbs for poison? I mean if they find none."

Ben shrugged. "It could prove that the tea didn't kill Mrs. Worth, at any rate. That might help. And the tea is the suspicious thing right now. Well, that and the crystal ball."

"Suspicious? Why would it be? It was only an ornament," I told him. "Nothing more than that."

"I agree with you," Ben assured me. "Yet Mr. Richard swears that it vanished as though by magic."

I had not heard that. "What?"

Ben raised his eyebrows. "Didn't I tell you? I heard someone say that the crystal was one reason Mr. Richard

Worth keeps insisting Moll is a witch. He says she left the glass ball on the mantel in Mrs. Worth's bedroom, but when he looked for it just after her death, it had mysteriously vanished, as though summoned back to Moll by some sinister spell."

I tried to remember whether I had seen the little lavender orb on the day that Ben found Mrs. Worth dead, but for the life of me I could not recall whether it had still been on the mantel or not. "I think that's all foolishness," I said at last. "But I also believe we might have a chance at helping Moll if we can find that bag of herbs. If only we could retrieve it from the house, and if someone knowing could examine it—"

"Dr. Blackthorn," Ben said at once, sitting up very straight. "He would be the very person! If there are tests that would reveal such a poison, he would surely know all about it. He is a brilliant man, and learned in all fields. He's one of the cleverest fellows in the colonies."

"Would he help us?" I asked.

Ben considered. "I think it's very likely he would," he said slowly. "He is no sour, ranting Puritan, no gullible and easily fooled believer in witches and goblins, but a level-headed natural philosopher who is interested not just in the study of medicine but in all other subjects. I've heard him speak learnedly of botany, of curious minerals, and of the electricity—he can make sparks leap with a woolen cloth and a rod of amber! I know the doctor pretty well and would have no fear of approaching him. If we can fetch the cloth pouch from the Worth house, I will undertake to carry it to the doctor and tell him what we want."

The problem then became how to retrieve the bag. I remembered right well where it was—I had tossed it into the pail that held all the kinds of kitchen slops no one wished to feed to the hogs. I had not emptied that into the midden in the back of the yard, as I usually did every other day or so, and since there was no other servant to do that task, I supposed the bag still must lie there in the kitchen, unless a constable had removed it.

It would take but a moment to look for it, if we could just seize that moment in which to do the looking. However, Ben understood that a fat, slow, and stupid deputy was sleeping in the front parlor of the house every night, keeping guard. "What is he guarding?" I asked.

Ben shrugged. "Although Mr. Richard claims he thinks you stole the iron box of money, he doesn't know for sure. It may still be hidden in the house, and so they are taking no chances. Listen, for I'm sure we can get you in and out safely if I can lure that fat and silly constable into the street. Here's how we'll do it."

Ben was clever, and I hoped his plot would work. We agreed that we would have to risk it. That evening, as dusk fell, we made our way quickly down Orange Street toward Boston Neck, with me in my concealing black bonnet, slumping to make myself look shorter and keeping my eyes low so that no one could glimpse my features.

In a way I wished that we had thought of our scheme in time to have done it in the fog, when we would have had better cover. Many people in that part of town knew me by sight, and the last thing we wanted was to rouse a hue and cry. However, though the sky was clear above us, with early stars already gleaming overhead, a smartly cold wind gusted and swept the dust in billows from the streets, so that none of the few huddled, hurrying people in the streets gave us so much as a second glance.

Even so, we took to side lanes and back passageways well before drawing near to Mr. Richard's house, and we did that far to the back, beyond the end of his garden, through a patch of head-high dry and rustling weeds. We pushed through some overgrown hedges and so at last came to Mrs. Worth's backyard, near the refuse heap. The chickens had all been removed, and in the dying light the coop looked forlorn and empty. "We'll meet there after you get it," Ben said softly in my ear, pointing toward the chicken coop.

I did not answer, for my heart was in my mouth. I do not agree with Constable Wilkes that all girls are silly, weak, and frightened of their shadows, but now that we were actually upon the spot, I was beginning to dread the next few minutes. I told myself that Moll needed me to do this, and that seemed to give me a little spirit. *'Tis not being free of fear that makes one brave,* I thought. *'Tis being afraid to do what you must do—and making yourself do that thing anyway, as best you can.*

Ben and I slipped up to the rear of the house, and I tried the back door, but as we had expected, it proved to be locked up tight. "Listen," Ben murmured, and from inside came the horrible rattle of a man's deep snore. "I'll wake him up," Ben said. "Be ready." He circled around to the front, and as we had planned, in the deep dusk he pounded up the steps onto the porch, making as much noise as he possibly could, and banged thunderously on the door. I hid around the corner, peeking out just enough to see what was happening so I should know when my cue to act should occur. A man opened the door almost at once. From where I hid, I could not well see him, but I could hear his angry, rasping voice: "What's all this uproar? What are you about, boy?"

"Sir, sir!" Ben cried in a disguised, high-pitched voice, leaping from the porch before the man could possibly get a good look at him, and then running to the dark street, beckoning wildly with waving arms. "This way! Help! Help! Come quick!" And he went dashing off into the gloom.

I pressed close to the house, waiting to see if Ben's trick would really work. I flinched away as the fat constable stepped out into the yard and darted a suspicious glance all round, but he must not have seen me. The man hesitated for only a moment. "Who are you? What's wrong?"

From the darkness far down the street Ben screeched, "Hurry, sir, make haste!"

As soon as the constable, a large, ungainly man who walked a bit like a duck, waddled off after him, I dashed up the steps, holding up my skirts, and into the house. A lone candle in the parlor gave a dim yellow light, and the passage and kitchen were in darkness, but I knew the house like my own hand, and it took me but a moment to dart into the kitchen, drop to my knees, and feel around in the nasty slop pail. It stank of stale rot, and my stomach lurched as I felt soft, slimy things, but I also found the cloth bag and clutched it as I rose to my feet and ran back to the front door. I stepped onto the porch—and at once I heard a bellow of outrage from the constable! "Hey there! Stop! Stop in the name of the King's law!"

Small chance of that. The constable had given up his

chase of Ben after only a moment. I heard the man gasping and panting as he ran in a wobbly way for the steps, cutting off my only clear way of escape. Instead, as he mounted up the steps to the porch, I leaped over the far rail, landed hard on my feet and my outstretched hand with a jolt that made my teeth click together, and then scrambled back up, running in the direction of Boston Neck, the guardhouses, and the mainland. The big-bellied constable had been taken by surprise when I jumped, and he had to scramble back down the steps. I heard him stumble and yelp in annoyance or pain. The man's hoarse and furious voice shouted again, and then I heard Ben's screeching shout from somewhere behind him: "There he goes, Constable Potts! I see the rogue! Away to the right!"

And being no fool, I cut to the left.

"Where is he?" yelled the constable as I skidded to a stop and shrank into the dark shadow of a huge old elm, trying to press myself right into the bark and become invisible. Though I could not have been inside for more than a minute, it seemed to me the night had grown perceptibly darker—and I was thankful for that. Then, suddenly, I could hear the constable's footsteps, not a dozen paces away! If he but turned and walked toward the house, I would be trapped—I was grateful that he had not had the wit to seize a lantern before answering Ben's knock. "Hang it!" the constable wheezed. "Where is the little rogue?"

Then Ben cut in again, disguising his voice so he sounded like an old man: "I see him! There! There! He's away down Orange Street, heading for town! Hurry and you'll have him! He's up again and off! There he runs—there he runs, he's turned to the left! A rascally redheaded boy of twelve! Don't you see him?"

"Stop where you stand, you infernal brat!" I heard the man's heavy footsteps running in a ponderous drumming, but they were going away from the house and away from my hiding place. The constable's threatening voice faded to a far-off bellow as he followed Ben's false trail. I hurried around to the backyard and crouched behind the hen coop, where Ben and I had agreed to meet. A moment later, when Ben touched my shoulder, I gave a violent start, but I just managed to keep myself from crying aloud. By that time it was nearly full night, and I could see Ben only as a silhouette in the darkness.

"Did you find it?" he whispered.

"I have it here." I drew a deep, shaky breath, clenching the bag tight in my fist. "That man almost caught me!"

"Aye, 'twas a narrow scrape. Obadiah Potts is fat and slow of thought, but he can be a confounded nuisance. Come on.

This part of the town will soon grow too hot for us!"

We hastened away, going again by a crooked route through lanes and alleys, and at last Ben let us back into the shop, through the back door. "I have to go home now," he said as I took off the stove the bucket in which I heated water. The fire had burned low, and the remaining water was only warm now, but after grubbing about in all that smelly refuse and running through the evening, I needed to wash my hands and sponge myself. Ben gallantly hauled the bucket of water into the back room for me and said, "My father will have my hide if I'm too late for supper. Give me the herb bag, and tomorrow I'll see that Dr. Blackthorn has it."

I passed it to him.

"Faugh!" he said, wrinkling his nose. "It stinks!"

I fetched a piece of paper—there were thousands to choose from!—and Ben wrapped the pouch up in it. I asked, "How will you explain it to the doctor? How will you say you got hold of it?"

"I'll think of a good story to tell him," Ben said with a grin. "I'm a bit of a writer, you know. Did I tell you I write poems?"

I was washing my hands, as well as I could, in the warm water. "When you come tomorrow, bring a bit of soap if you can. Did I know you made some poems? Yes, you told me so. And you said your brother printed them and sold them."

Ben looked almost dreamy. To my surprise he began to recite:

"I have a tale of tragedy,
That chanced upon the sea,
A storm that took five Christian souls,
And one whole family—"

"Ben," I said gently. "Supper."

"Yes," he said, blinking himself out of his momentary trance. He sighed. "Oh, well. My father does not like my poems either. He tells me that only fools write verses, because there is no money in them and a man cannot eat literary fame. I suppose he is right about that, though he did hurt my feelings at the time he said it. But Father knows what he is talking about when he says the way to wealth does not lead through the pages of a poetry book! Good night."

He left me alone, and then with a torn rag, one of the cleaning rags in a pile in the storage room, I sponge-bathed as well as I could without soap and in the darkness. Quickly I tossed the dirty water out the back door and then got ready for bed. In my little closet I lit my tallow candle again, and to get my mind off the risk we had taken and off my worries about Moll and her troubles, I took up the story of Robinson Crusoe, who had by that time made for himself some clothing of goatskin, built himself a kind of home, planted a garden, explored his little island, and even tamed a parrot and taught it to say words of pity to him.

By the time I began to nod into sleep, poor Robinson Crusoe's stay on his deserted island had stretched out into years. After perhaps an hour of reading I at last drifted off asleep, hoping that my own troubles would not be so persistent.

The next morning I awoke in cold darkness, wrapped tight in my blankets and wondering why the cubbyhole smelled so ill, a stale stench like grease left too long on the stove. Then I felt the book, open and spread out on my chest, and realized that I had gone to sleep reading. The candle had guttered out, and what I could smell was the burned tallow that had pooled in the holder. Had I allowed Mrs. Worth's candles to burn away to nothing like that, she would have had a harsh word and a hard hand for me.

I felt the stub of the candle and pinched off the long, curled, black wick so the ash wouldn't keep it from catching fire then I found the tinderbox and struck a spark. With the candle so short, it was hard to light, but at last I got a little orange flame going, and in its feeble, flickering, sickly glow I hastily dressed myself. Ben had showed me where more tallow candles were stored, and I took one to replace my burned-out stub. As I pried the old one from its holder, I wrinkled my nose. Tallow candles are always stinky and greasy—if you get a splotch of melted tallow on your clothing, it will never come out again. Fleetingly, I wished that Mr. James were rich enough to afford good beeswax candles, which are cleaner to burn, do not smell so bad, and give a brighter and clearer light.

Ben came while the world was still dark, as he had done the day before, and again he brought a breakfast, which we shared in haste. He said that he would be about early, selling the newspapers—though they were printed each Monday, they were on sale throughout the week, and Ben had told me that demand for this week's issue, with its story of an unnatural death, had been quite high. He said that as he sold the papers, he would be sure to take a route that would let him duck into Dr. Blackthorn's house with the bag of herbs.

Soon I slipped out and waited near the street door, shivering in the cold dawn until Mr. James appeared, and then I met him at the front, went in, made up the fire in the stove, and got busy with my chores. Ben left the shop at about eight thirty with a monstrous bundle of *Courant*s to sell, and soon the idle friends of Mr. James began to drift in, sit, laugh, and chatter. I thought privately that if Mr. James would devote but half the energy to printing that he spent in socializing, he would be a more successful man.

But I had scarcely any time to worry about that, for again I had to sweep out the whole shop, and then lug armfuls of firewood in from a large jumbled pile out back to refill the wood box beside the stove, and after that Mr. James thought up yet more tasks for me. I did them mechanically, without thinking of them much.

All of my worries hung on the doctor and what Ben could convince him to do for us. I only hoped that Ben had been right about Dr. Blackthorn, and that the doctor was clever enough to help Moll prove her innocence—yet not so clever that he could entrap Ben and me, for I supposed that in doing our best for Moll, we had bent, if not broken, all sorts of laws. My distraction soon enough ended, though, for in the early part of the afternoon Ben came running into the shop.

The second I saw his stricken expression, my heart gave a painful thud.

Something, his look told me, had gone horribly wrong.

ℭ Eight ℥

Though a brother, he considered himself as my master,
and me as his apprentice . . .
—The Autobiography of Benjamin Franklin

Before Ben and I could snatch a moment to speak to each other, James Franklin turned from the press and confronted his brother angrily. "You have had time to do your errand five times over! Thank you so much for deciding to favor us with your presence once again, Master Franklin. Here, now, take this and be quicker about it!" Mr. James reached to a counter and then handed Ben a twice-folded paper.

"Couldn't I just—," Ben began.

James cut him short: "You can *just* do your job; that's what you can *just* do! Listen now, and remember what I want. We have to have more paper and ink. Take this order to Crawford's—you know the place—and wait until Mr. Crawford himself gives you an answer."

"Yes, but—"

James punched him on the arm, not really hard, but in annoyance, not in play. "Close your mouth and open your ears for a change! Tell him we need all this by next Monday, when we print the next issue. I must know if he can supply us with all we need by then, and if he cannot, I must make other arrangements today. If he is out of his office, wait there until he comes in. Remember, I must have an answer from him, not from anyone else, because last time his fool of a chief clerk forgot all about our paper until it was nearly too late to do us any good. Don't stand there gawping! Off with you!" Ben had been giving me an anguished look, but James roughly shoved him along toward the door. He even aimed a kick at Ben as Ben turned, but he missed. The young idlers laughed at that.

As I watched Ben run off on his errand, I was on fire to know what the trouble was, but I had no way of learning it. To make matters worse Mr. James settled into a chair and in a loud, angry voice began to mock his younger brother to his friends: "He is such a tiresome lad. Always daydreaming and getting into trouble! I wonder my father hasn't tied him in a sack, like an unwanted puppy, and thrown him in the Mill Pond to drown before this!"

I had to bite my tongue to keep from protesting

Mr. James's harsh manner and angry words, and I began to feel sorry for Ben—he and I were not so different.

"Drowning him would never work," one of his friends said, laughing. "Your little brother swims like a fish!"

Another one said, "That's true. I remember well seeing him splashing in the pond one summer day a year or so ago. He was lying flat on his back in the water—I know not how he kept from sinking—and holding tight on to the string of a kite, which towed him from one bank to the other, like a ship with a flying sail!"

"Aye," said James in a surly tone. "Ben's always been a great one for swimming. And who ever profited by swimming? He should be kept busy all the time, because the moment he has leisure, he finds some trouble to stir up. Did I ever tell you the story of how he got into so much disfavor with our father when he was about ten? He and some of his young friends always went a-fishing for eels in the pond in the summers—a whole rough, good-for-nothing gang of them. They had their favorite spot, but by going there every day, they eventually trampled the shore up into mud and made it all a mere quagmire."

One of the others laughed. "Yes, I know that story! Young Ben decided that what the lads needed was a fishing pier to give them a solid place to stand where they could keep their feet dry."

James nodded. "And so he organized them all, half a dozen or more of idle young rogues and rascals, and they found a great pile of rocks and lugged them one by one down to the shore. It must have been prodigiously hard work, because these were substantial stones, not cobbles. I can just imagine them, slaving away like a line of ants! They built their pier, all right, there along the muddy shore of the Mill Pond and out a few feet into the water—I saw it together with my father, and I will even admit they did a good job of it, and had made themselves a fine dry place to fish from. The trouble was that they had taken all the stone from a building site."

The man who had heard the story before gave a great bark of laughter, sounding like a hoarse seal. "Ben Franklin a thief, by thunder! He should have stood a day in the stocks for that little caper!"

James nodded. "Yes, they had stolen building material. All those stones had been meant to go into the foundation of a house! When the builders came the next morning, they found their whole pile had been pilfered. But it had not gone far—all of the rascals were just little boys, and they could not have carried or even hauled away with a wagon such heavy weights, at least not for a very long way—and in looking around, the builders soon enough discovered exactly what had happened to their property, for there was Ben, proud as any popinjay, along with some other young thieves, standing on their new stone pier and happily a-fishing for flounders!"

"I'll wager he got a good tanning for that," one of the men said, shaking his head and grinning. "My father would have taken a rawhide strap and would have had the hide off my backside had I tried such a trick!"

"Oh, yes, you'd think he'd be smartly whipped," agreed James in a disgruntled, cross voice, "but Father has always been too easy on him." Looking sour and disappointed, James Franklin shook his head. "No, no real beating for my clever little rascal of a brother. For punishment my father gave Benjamin only a few mild swats on his haunches with a thin little rod, together with a long paternal sermon on the eighth commandment."

"Well, I am sure he will come to no good in the end," the first young idler said, stretching his arms and giving a tremendous yawn. "These clever boys always end up in jail or worse."

I waited most of the day for Ben to return, worried and anxious, and all the while imagining all sorts of horrible things that he might have wanted to tell me. Had Dr. Blackthorn discovered poison in the herbs, after all? Had something terrible happened to Moll Bacon, locked away in her prison cell? Had some other disaster befallen that I had not even thought of? I was so quiet and preoccupied that Mr. James asked at one point if I felt ill, and I said no, I was just thinking of what chore to do next.

"Things are pretty well in hand here now. You can go if you wish. Take the rest of the day," he said, glancing round at the pendulum clock, which showed the time as twenty-five minutes to four. "There is not much left to do in the shop. However, tomorrow will be a busy day—Fridays always are, for that's when we begin setting type for Monday's paper— so be here spot on time, Mercy. Oh, and tomorrow before you leave, I will give you your first week's pay as well. Remind me of that if I should forget."

I could not well argue with my employer that I did not want to leave, and yet I had nowhere to go. After wasting a few more minutes lingering about, pretending to dust and tidy up a few last-minute things, I at last walked out of the shop and down Queen Street, feeling that all eyes were on me, that suspicion was all about me, and that at any moment I would feel a constable's hard hand grasp my shoulder and a stern official voice call out my name.

The only possible refuge I could think of was the tumble-down hut in Tanner's Lane—but when I came near it, I saw

men working on it, busily taking it to pieces! I supposed that
Mr. Richard had investigated and decided he could not rent
the place out, and so he had instead sold it for the price of
the lumber. After one glance I looked away and passed on by,
willing the workmen not to notice me and trying to shrink
modestly down inside my Quaker dress so they would have
no reason to look my way.

Feeling truly lost and all alone, I wandered up and down
the streets of town, moving fast enough so that people might
be fooled into thinking I was running some urgent errand.
The day grew steadily colder and colder as I hurried about
aimlessly until twilight came, and then, with no other place
of refuge to head for, I slipped back to the shop.

It was dark, closed and locked up tight for the night.
I went round to the back with some faint hope that Ben
might have had the wit to leave me a way in, but the back
door was bolted as well. It was going to be a freezing night,
and I had neither coat nor shawl to protect me. The evening
wind cut through my dress like a sharp knife slicing through
hasty pudding.

Feeling miserable and hugging my arms around myself, I
huddled as well as I could into the doorway and sat deject-
edly there shivering with my heart down in my shoes, trying
hard to think of some shift, some trick, some way of finding

a place to stay where I would have hopes of not freezing quite to death.

Mrs. Worth had always kept me close at home. Though I could find my way around the town, after a fashion, I had not much experience of Boston and hardly knew where to begin to look for shelter. I did not dare return to Mrs. Worth's house after the narrow escape we had faced the night before. Even if the same slow constable were still sleeping there, I could not hope to evade him again. True, there was also the deserted hen coop, but it offered little protection from the cold wind, and it was filthy with chicken droppings as well. Then, too, I did not want to be in that neighborhood, where any one of ten or twelve women friends of Mrs. Worth who lived nearby might recognize me come morning.

The wind grew keener, and no matter how tightly I tried to hug my own arms, it soon became clear to me that if I waited there in the doorway, I would surely perish of cold. I did not want to spend the night in the privy, for anyone happening along might feel the need to use it and discover me. I had about made up my mind to get up and simply walk to and fro all night, just to keep some spark of warmth in my limbs, hoping that I would not fall down dead from frostbite and trying to avoid the night watch.

But then I heard someone moving around in the street.

I dashed to the corner and peeked out, but I could see no one in the murky darkness, for full night had fallen by then, and the icy white moon, only a crescent that evening, did not even show in the black gap of sky I could see between the roofs of the buildings. Then I heard someone moving in the shop.

Was it Ben? Or had Mr. James come back and let himself in the back door? From where I hid, I could not tell. After a moment or two a dim glow seeped out of the one window, but it quickly vanished as someone inside drew the curtain. Surely, I thought, it must be Ben—why would Mr. James Franklin come sneaking into his own establishment at night? It made all the sense in the world, and in the cold I could almost persuade myself to believe the supposition.

The biting wind was so sharp that I could not wait for very long. I went on tiptoe to the back door, tried it again, found it unbolted, opened it as silently as a mouse might creep across a heavy blanket, and sneaked inside. My fingers were numb, and my nose ached. The stove had not been long out in the shop, and the warmth there actually stung my cheeks and ears. A single tallow candle burned in a holder set low on one of the shelves, a good distance beneath the covered window. The angle of the light made distorted, ghostly shadows on the floor. No one was in the room; if

Mr. James was in the shop, he was out front. I decided to nip into my hiding place and keep still. Gliding my feet as silently as I could, I stooped to open the low door.

And then I yelped in alarm as it *flew* open, as if it had been done by a conjuring trick or a ghost! From inside the compartment someone holding a second candle lunged out at me!

"Shh!" The dark figure raised up, and I recognized Ben, the light from his candle making him look strange. He nipped it out, and then he was just a black shape against the dim light from the other candle that burned on the shelf.

"Where have you been?" I asked hotly, but in a whisper. "You were away so long that James sent me home—"

"I know, I know," Ben said apologetically. "I came to see if you had hidden in your room there before he left. Oh, I have left another dress, this one black, and some other clothing for you there now—my friend found them for me, and they should fit you at least as well as those—"

I grabbed him by the shoulders and shook him. "Ben Franklin, I knew the moment I saw you when you came back to the shop today that something is dreadfully wrong. Tell me what it is!"

"All right, all right!" He turned, leaned over, and blew out the remaining candle. "But let's talk in the dark. If the night watch should come through the back alley and spy a light—"

"It's dark now," I said. "Tell me!"

"First, Dr. Blackthorn was not at his home when I called there—an odd thing, because he usually does not call upon patients until after two. But his people insisted that he had been called away for a sudden illness, and they refused to tell me where—I could leave a note for him, they said, as if that would have done the least good! Anyway, it was hard, but I learned from a servant that he had been called to Mr. Richard Worth's house. It seems Mr. Richard is grievously sick."

I stared hard, though all I could see was darkness. "Sick? What's wrong with him? How is he sick?"

"With a painful sharp griping of the guts and horrible vomiting. He says the pain is terrible, doubling him over into a knot and tearing at his innards."

"That sounds like the same illness Mrs. Worth had—poisoning!" I exclaimed.

"Aye," said Ben in a grim voice. "That's what I thought as well. And so as soon as I learned where Dr. Blackthorn had gone, I pelted away down Orange Street as fast as my legs would move me and waited about until I saw the doctor come out of Mr. Worth's house. I ran to the side of the road, and as he came riding by, I waved him down—he was riding his big gray mare—and told him about the herbs—"

"What story did you give him? You didn't tell him about me?"

"No, no," Ben said placatingly. "Give me more credit than that! I blamed a mysterious redheaded boy, who I said had been sent by Moll Bacon's friends to seek out the bag as proof that she had done no poisoning, and who had asked me to take the evidence to the doctor because it is well known that I esteem him. And he believed me, because that constable last night swore by everything he held dear that he had come within mere inches of running down a redheaded sneaking rogue who had slipped into the house by some secret way!"

"Don't sound so pleased with yourself for fooling the fellow," I snapped. "'Tis a sin to tell a lie."

Ben snorted in derision. "Then the constable is a great sinner, for from what I heard, he has transformed his silly blundering after us in the darkness to an epic battle worthy of Homer himself!"

"Who is Homer?"

"Who is—why, Homer was a learned old Greek gentleman who wrote tales of war and monsters. He's famous, and—but never mind for the moment." Ben took a breath and then said, "Let me finish. The doctor took the bag of herbs and said he would read in his books to see if there is any kind of method of determining whether it holds, or held, arsenic. He told me he thought that especially since the herbs were still damp, such a test would be possible. Arsenic has a foul, sharp scent, he said, a little like garlic but more piercing and unpleasant. And if poison is present, and it is the more common type of arsenic, when he dries the herbs carefully and completely he should be able to see a fine white powder."

"Well," I said, looking as it were for a light in the darkness, "at least we know that if Mr. Richard is being poisoned too, it could be none of Moll Bacon's doing. She never gave him a cup of her herbal tea, and she must have already been in her prison cell when he fell ill."

"No, but—well, there's more," said Ben's voice in the darkness. "Bad news, I fear." He sounded strangely reluctant to me.

I steeled myself, as though anticipating a blow. "Tell it, then."

For perhaps half a minute or so Ben sat silent, as if gathering his thoughts, and all became so still that I could hear the slow tick of the clock in the farther room, and the creaks and pings the stove made as it cooled. Then, quietly, he said, "This is the worst of it, then. Sometime today, as the constables were searching Moll Bacon's house for the third or fourth time, one of them stood on a chair and looked at the rafters—they run across the rooms, you know, and only part of them is covered with boards to make a sort of loft room—"

"Benjamin Franklin, stop all this and simply tell me what they found!" I exclaimed. "Arsenic?"

"No," Ben said slowly. "Remember that little glass ball you told me she left in Mrs. Worth's room?"

I felt cold, but it had nothing to do with the weather. I could picture the small, lavender-colored sphere quite well in my mind's eye. "Yes?"

"That ball was hidden, and well hidden, in her house. A man was standing on a chair and feeling around when he discovered it resting atop one of the rafters, jammed hard against the slope of the roof."

"It might not have even been the same one," I said.

"But they took it to Mr. Worth's house, because his son had first told them about it," Ben said. "And David Worth took a good long look at it and swears he thinks this is the same one."

"That doesn't make any sense."

"I know it doesn't," replied Ben with a sigh. "And though I don't believe in witches and magic—well, how could that glass ball somehow vanish from Mrs. Worth's mantel and reappear in Moll Bacon's house? How could it do that, if not by magic?"

"I don't remember when I last saw it," I said. "I could have taken it away, though I didn't, or you could have, or Mr. David, or the doctor, or the undertakers, or even Mr. Richard's cook."

"But why?" asked Ben.

And for that I had no answer.

∽ Nine ∾

*If it does not deserve the name poison,
what else could it be called?
—The Pennsylvania Gazette*

"Mr. Richard insists that Moll Bacon has bewitched him into his illness," Ben told me solemnly. He lowered his voice to little more than a hushed whisper and went on: "His tale is that she has used some foul, wicked magic to cause him to fall ill. The glass orb he calls an evil eye, and he declares that she has used it somehow to send a devilish spirit to torment him. He flatly denies that he could have been poisoned, for he has eaten and drunk nothing out of the ordinary, and all in the house have had the same food and drink as he. None of them are sick."

I shook my head in wonder at such plain, stubborn ignorance. "What does the doctor say to that? Surely he can't think that the illness is all caused by magic!"

"No, of course he does not," said Ben. He made his voice low and rumbling, like that of Dr. Blackthorn: "'A physical disease must be the effect of a physical cause,' says he. He tells me he has sternly warned Mr. Worth not to put off calling him if he grows worse—and not to think himself healed if he feels somewhat better tomorrow. 'It's as bad to be well too early as sick too late,' he says, which seems to me a fine and practical thought—"

"Oh, you talk like an almanac." I could not hold back a great, gaping yawn, for with all the excitement, coupled with the periods of work and boredom of the last few days, I was weary indeed. "Ben, it's late. Should you not be home by this time?"

Ben stood. Now that my eyes had grown somewhat used to the darkness, I could barely see his shape as he moved silently to the back wall and carefully drew the curtain from the window. The dimmest possible glimmer of moonlight showed me his profile as he stared out at the alley. "Yes, you're right. I should slip home before I'm missed. Wrap up well tonight, for it's going to be very cold. I shouldn't be surprised to see frost painting our windows come morning."

"We need to speak with Moll Bacon somehow," I said.

Ben let the curtain fall back in place. "That will be a

problem. She is held pretty closely, I hear. I will think on it, though."

I heard his hand fumbling at the door handle, and before he could leave, I said, "Thank you, Ben. Whatever happens, I will always remember how you helped me."

"It is nothing," he said modestly. "At least it breaks the monotony of being an apprentice! Good night, now."

He sneaked out, giving me a faint and fleeting glimpse of the muted moonlit alley, and I locked the door after him before creeping into my little sleeping compartment. I felt very tired, and I was so much disturbed in mind that I did not, for a change, take up my book. Instead I lay swaddled in my blankets, my head teeming with impossible plots and schemes to find some way, any way, of talking to Moll Bacon.

James Franklin had not been jesting when he told me that the next day would be a busy one. The printing shop was like a beehive lifted, shaken, and turned topsy-turvy. I must admit that as I began the day, my foolish vanity was punctured, for no one even noticed the "new" black dress I wore, which I thought far more suitable and better fitting than the gray. That morning Ben had brought me a little earthenware pot of soft soap, and though it was not the best thing to use on soiled garments, I judged that I could at least wash my gray dress that evening, wring it out, and hang it to dry from a cord that we strung in my sleeping-closet. Then if Ben could just smuggle an iron in to me, I would have a grand wardrobe. Having two different dresses to wear, and one of them black enough to serve as the belated mourning for my dead mother and father, made me feel quite wealthy.

As we all worked, Ben's quick dexterity with his fingers impressed me. He could set type almost as fast as a person could talk, selecting the metal letters from a huge compartmented tray, sliding them one by one into a form, and making up line after line of type, and all backward! He put his brother to shame, for James took a far longer time to compose the lines, and as often as not he would make a mistake that he would not catch until he had printed a proof, a trial sheet. Ben's sharp eyes would almost always catch such errors before the type was locked into the form, and his pages rarely had so much as a letter out of alignment, let alone the wrong letter, or the right letter in the wrong place, or one turned upside down.

I do not remember all the stories in that issue of the *New-England Courant,* except I do recall that James had written another blistering, ridiculing attack on smallpox inoculation, denouncing Dr. Boylston and proclaiming all the two hundred or so folks he had inoculated, every single one of us, fools and dunces. He heaped withering scorn, too, on Cotton Mather, for as Ben observed, such controversies stirred up the readers and sold newspapers.

By late afternoon the paper had been run off in proof and the printed pages were hanging on a rack a-drying. Mr. James seemed so pleased with the great public stir the paper was bound to make that he proposed to make another early afternoon of it, and he gave me the pennies that he had promised me for my labor. In the midst of all my woe and confusion, I must tell you that receiving the clinking coins from his hand gave me a sense of pride such as I had rarely before known. *It is a fine thing to make your own way in the world*, I decided, and I liked it.

When we had a moment alone, Ben said, "I see James gave you hard clinking money. I thought he would try to palm off some notes."

"Paper money?" I asked. "What's wrong with that?"

"Nothing, except you have to be careful. Some notes from the other colonies are worth only half what their face value says. James would rather take eggs for a subscription to the *Courant* than a note from Virginia! But you have good coins, so what are you going to do with them?"

"Pay you back with some of them," I said, "and save the rest."

Ben nodded his approval. "Saving is wise. They say that saving a penny is the same as earning one. But as for paying me back, don't even think of it, for you owe me nothing. Listen, now, for I think I may have schemed a way for you to see Moll Bacon, if you dare—but I have to warn you, it is dangerous. There is a chance someone could see through your disguise."

"What is this scheme of yours?" I asked.

"Listen: It is a usual thing for friends of prisoners to send them small gifts, food and blankets and such, for their comfort. What could be more probable than some woman whom Moll helped while she gave birth to her children should send Moll a pot of jam and a warm nightgown? I can find those easily, and you can claim to be the bearer of the gifts. That might get you five minutes with her."

"It could work," I said. "I could claim, even, that my mother has sent the presents."

"But you will not have much time with her," Ben warned. "Think of the three things you must ask her, and decide which is the most important of those. Ask that first, then the next most important, and so to the last. And if you wish, you might write these down, and perhaps a few more questions as well, so that you can best use your time."

"That is a good idea," I said. When I had a moment of leisure to do it, I sat in a quiet corner and with a pen began to scribble the questions that I most wanted answered:

1. **How can you explain the glass ball found by the constables in your house?**
2. **What herbs did you give me to brew for tea?**
3. **What could prove that you had naught to do with Mrs. Worth's death?**

So much did I concentrate my attention on this task that I did not even notice Mr. James passing by until he asked in a joking voice, "Well, Mercy, are you writing a piece for the *Courant*?"

I had the presence of mind not to yank the paper away, knowing that would only make him ask to read it. "No, sir," I said. "I was trying to cipher a sum."

"What sum?" he said, grinning at me.

I could feel myself blushing. "I have always wanted silk garters," I said softly. "My mother thinks they are sinful, but I would so like to save enough to buy a pair. They must be very dear."

"Silk garters." He went away chuckling, and I knew full

well that soon enough he would entertain his friends with the story of the proud Quaker girl who, the minute she had two pennies to rub together, wanted nothing more than the silly vanity of silk garters.

That afternoon, when we left the shop, Ben took me to a nearby place, the used-clothing shop where his friend worked for his father, and we bought an old nightgown for twopence. That was a generous price, since it was so worn it would hardly serve even as cleaning rags, but Ben judged that jailers would not look too closely at a feminine garment. Ben then bought a little pot of strawberry preserves, and we made our way back to the prison in Queen Street. I have said that I did not like the look of the place. It had a little plot of earth between it and the street, all overgrown with pigweed and burdock, and the weathered, dark walls with their ponderous ironbound door had all the harsh, unforgiving attitude of the old Puritan fathers of the town, or so it seemed to me. But we went to it with a fair show of boldness. Ben acted as though he were my guide, and I pretended to be almost too shy to live, and so he took on the responsibility of telling the guards our business. They knew Ben well, since they saw him about in the street almost every day, and our request did not seem to strike them as much out of the ordinary. They acted as though it were only a trifle, a matter of course, and an elderly turnkey with a sour, wrinkled face like a dried-up apple took me back to Moll's cell. "Be brief," he said in a creaking voice.

Moll was sitting forlorn on her bed—which was just a couple of rough planks nailed together and slung down from the splintery wooden wall by two chains, with only a coarse blanket, not fit for a horse, covering it. The midwife had been slumped back with her arms folded across her chest, her shoulders resting against the wall, her head down, but she looked up with her smoldering dark eyes as I approached the bars. Her expression did not change a whit. She said not a word. I had to admire her coolness, for in her place I would have cried out from mere surprise at seeing a familiar face in that terrible prison.

"Mistress Bacon," I said in a low and very hesitant voice before Moll might greet me and give away my imposture, "I am sure you do not recognize me, but you brought me into the world. My name is Mercy Dyer, and on the day when my mother, Charity Dyer, gave birth to me, and when her life was despaired of, you saved us both. She has told me many times of the quantities of blood she lost, and how at the end, when I was safely delivered and she was weak but still aware, you were covered from arms to shoulders in dripping gore—"

"I will be at the end of the corridor," the guard said hastily, his wrinkled old face turning a pale shade of apple green. He left us and went far enough away so that Moll and I could speak quietly together without his overhearing.

"Men," Moll said quietly, shaking her head. "They call themselves brave, and mayhap they can abide to face an armed enemy in battle, but when women speak of childbirth, they lose their nerve altogether—that was clever of you, Patience."

"'Twas not my idea, but another's. First, take these." I passed my gifts to Moll, and as she stood close, I whispered: "Moll, we are trying to help you. I need you to answer some questions for me."

"Ask away, Patience"—Moll's hatchet face softened in a surprisingly gentle smile—"I mean, Mercy Dyer."

I asked the first question, and she said in slow, thoughtful tones, "It must be some trick of those who wish me in prison. I cannot see how the glass ball could have been found in my house. I had only the one, a bauble that one of my patients gave me years ago. You saw where I placed it, and there upon the mantel in Mrs. Abedela's room I left it. If it was moved back to my home, be sure a human hand did it and no spirit. If you could find who returned the glass ball, you might go a great way toward learning who poisoned Mrs. Abedela."

I nodded and read the second question: What was in the pouch of herbs? Moll smiled and shook her head. "Nay, child, I will not tell my secrets. I will say that only innocent health-giving herbs were in the mixture. To tell you the whole recipe—well, you would have to be my apprentice before I would do that, for 'tis a mystery of my profession."

And then the third question, to see if Moll had any notion of what might prove her innocence. After a considering pause Moll said, "Child, if I knew of a sure way to clear my name, I would not this instant be sitting in a cell in Boston Prison. I know of no way of proving my innocence without proving someone else's guilt." She fell silent, pondering for a few moments, before she began again: "If—but no, that is something I cannot ask."

"What?" I said urgently.

"Well . . . they have been asking me about Mrs. Worth's iron box of money. I never even set eyes upon it, but it is missing. If it could be found, then some suspicion might be lifted from me. But I do not know how you would even begin to—"

At that moment the shriveled old guard interrupted from his end of the corridor, "That's long enough. Say your good-byes and get you gone, girl."

I had to obey, though I was far from satisfied. At least, I

thought, it was good to know that Moll was safe and whole, though she had looked despairing when I first saw her in that awful cell. And I would have to thank Ben for his suggestion that I write down what I needed to know. Without the list, I would never have thought to ask all three questions. Indeed, the only trouble I could see was that not a single one of them had given me an answer that shed any light at all on the problem.

On Saturday, Mr. James was much surprised when Dr. Blackthorn called at the printing house, and positively astonished when the grave physician said he had not come to visit the master, but the apprentice. Mr. James threw up his hands and said he was stepping to a tavern nearby for a bite to eat and warned Ben to behave himself. The moment he was gone, Ben locked the front door and beckoned the doctor into the back room, and he called to me to come as well.

To my horror, when we all three were alone there in private, Ben said, "Doctor, this is Patience Martin, who has run away from her indentures because she heard Mr. Richard Worth planning to sell her into something very like slavery."

"Ah?" said the doctor, gazing at me with a sort of calm and speculative eye. "I recall seeing you, Miss Martin. Mr.

Richard has said so many ill things about you that I am sure you are a wonderfully pleasant young person—with Mr. Richard, I have found, 'tis best to take his opinions in the opposite."

"Please, sir," I said, "don't turn me in—"

"I? Turn you in?" he asked in surprise. Then he chuckled. "Stick out your tongue, Miss Martin. Yes, it looks like a healthy tongue. There, now I have medically examined you, and 'tis an old-established principle of law that a physician must hold the confidence of his patients, so I cannot possibly turn you in."

"Dr. Blackthorn is no friend of slavery, nor of bondage," Ben said. "What is it, sir? Why did you come to see me?"

"To tell you that the herbs in your cotton pouch were simple herbs, and that is all," the doctor said. "I found no least trace of arsenic or any other ill thing in them. However, there is a difficulty: How can you prove that the bag you gave me was the same that Moll Bacon gave to Mrs. Worth?"

Ben looked thunderstruck. "Why, Patience brewed the tea! She threw the bag into a slop pail, and she is the one who fetched it out again!"

"Aye," said the doctor, "and she dare not testify, for that would put her plump in the hands of the authorities. But let that be for the moment, Ben. I tell the two of you what I have told the constables, who choose not to listen or not to pay heed: Somehow Mrs. Worth was poisoned by arsenic. She must have taken the arsenic in on Thursday night, the night she died. I suspect that she was poisoned over a longer span of time, days at the least or perhaps even weeks, but the last fatal dose must have been given to her that night. Now, how was it given? I understand that she ate only bread and milk, and that both of those were wholesome. I confess I cannot conceive of any other way she could have been poisoned. Solve that riddle, and I think you may stand a chance to free your friend. Now I have to go, but I wish the two of you good luck. Farewell, Ben. Your servant, Miss Martin."

He bowed civilly and left us alone. I had, of course, already told Ben about my interview with Moll. Now I said, "The only thing we can now do to help is to tell the constables where that iron box is hidden."

"Surely they would have looked beneath the bed," Ben objected.

"Perhaps, but it couldn't have flown away—or have been spirited away," I told him.

Ben said, "But Mrs. Worth may have cleverly concealed it. What I would like to do is take a look for it ourselves. 'Tis a sorry thing to admit, but I am not sure I trust the constables right now. They are far too eager to serve the interests of Mr. Richard Worth, who has money and position, and to treat Moll ill, only because she has neither."

"How can we do that?" I asked. "That trick of shouting for help will never work a second time."

"No," Ben agreed. "But we have a bit of luck. Fat Constable Potts is still on watch, I have learned. I know full well that he is the soundest sleeper in all Christendom. If we can slip into the house at midnight, and if we take care to make little noise, we may search to our hearts' content without rousing him."

"It's too dangerous!"

"It's our best chance," he argued. "You know what they say: 'Plow deep while others sleep and you shall have corn to sell and corn to keep.'"

"What if he has locked the doors? He probably *will* lock them!"

"We will not need doors," Ben said firmly. "I have a scheme."

To tell the truth I liked not the sound of that—his last scheme had very nearly landed me in the hands of the law. But I heard him out. I will confess that on his first telling, it seemed to me a mad-headed, fantastical trick that had no chance of success. He was so enthusiastic, though, that I at last allowed him to persuade me that his plan stood some chance of success, and so, for the second time, we faced a night time expedition to Mrs. Worth's house, one that might either help us in our quest to free Moll Bacon—or else lead us into more trouble than we could handle.

❧ Ten ❧

Choose not to take by candle light.
—*Poor Richard's Almanac*

We could do nothing that night, and the next day, Sunday, was a day of rest. When Ben brought some food to me, he told me that our luck had turned for the worse: Someone finally had told James that the description of me in the broadsides was not accurate. However, as it was Sunday, at least James could do nothing about that for the time being, and Monday would be entirely taken up with finishing and distributing the next week's copy of the *Courant*.

"Did you take the blame?" I asked Ben.

He shrugged, wincing a little as he did so. "I was the one who set the type, so I had to do it."

I stared at him, not liking the way he had flinched. "Ben, tell me the truth. Did James beat you?"

"A few licks with a rod on my shoulders," he admitted.

"Tell your father!"

"'Twould do no good. Father says, 'He who loves well whips well.' In his view James is my master now." He reached up with his right hand and rubbed his left shoulder gingerly. "But this means we shall have to try our plan tonight. James will make me reset the handbill tomorrow or Tuesday, and this time I am sure he will read the finished copy, not just the rough proof."

"Did he not say anything about the proof being different the first time?"

Ben grinned. "Aye, but just as I had planned, I told him that I had dropped the form and spilled the type and reset all too hastily, looking at the wrong copy. He believed that I was so clumsy, because James will insist he's a better compositor than I am, despite all the clear evidence to the contrary. Get some sleep early, now. I will come after midnight, and we shall have to slink through the streets and avoid the watch."

Of course I could not go to church, and so I spent my Sunday morning reading in the Psalms and saying a prayer or two, and I hoped God would accept my goodwill as a substitute for hearing a sermon. I dreaded to think of going back to Mrs. Worth's house. It is a curious thing, but I have since noticed that, like me, many folks are fearful of something that is going to happen, so they suffer agonies in advance. And then when they have to do whatever unpleasant task it might be, they bear up well enough. If we could only borrow future courage from the actual event, I think, and use it while we are afraid beforehand, we might have an easier life of it.

I went to sleep clothed. Luckily, Ben had told me that morning that the weather had moderated. The cold, harsh northwesterly wind had slipped around to become a balmy southern breeze. The night would not be exactly warm, but at least the air would not nip our noses and cheeks!

Though I do not believe in any kind of magic, I do think we have odd talents that we never or only rarely use. I have a gift of sensing time fairly accurately, so that I woke in the dark quite suddenly just a few minutes before all the clocks in Boston tolled midnight. And not a minute later than that, Ben knocked on the low door of my sleeping room. I crept out and he handed me a lightweight bundle. "Carry this," he said. "I have cord and the rope coiled round my shoulders."

It felt like a sheet of silk, rolled up round a couple of sticks, and weighed nearly nothing at all. We went out and headed for the far side of town. The moon had grown a bit fatter, and it helped as we ducked here and there and kept a sharp eye out for the night watch. We heard one of them pacing his beat, whistling a low, mournful tune, and until he passed, we hid in a dark doorway. Dogs barked at us as we passed by their yards, but dogs are always barking, and no one seemed to pay them much mind. Again we crept up to Mrs. Worth's house from the rear, until we stood in the backyard.

Walking on tiptoe, we came near to the house, but before we were even close to the front, I could hear the long, rasping, window-rattling snore of Constable Potts. Ben had said he was a deep sleeper. I thought he must be, or else his own snoring would have awakened him. The very walls were all but shaking from the noise!

"Come," whispered Ben into my ear. "Now let's see if the wind will do."

It was a steady wind, not a full topsail gale, as my late father would have put it, but a constant breeze coming in from the south. It was near enough to what Ben wanted, and he tossed his bundles of cord and rope to the ground and took my parcel of silk and sticks. "Now," he said, "I think this is clever. A kite usually has one string; this has two. This one is the one I'll fly it by. The second, which you can see is tied here and here by slipknots, will unravel the silk from the middle of the kite, so I can make it fall whenever I wish.

I think I had better handle the kite. Let's get it into the air, and if the wind plays no tricks, you can go round to the far side of the house for the rest."

He quickly assembled the silk and the two crossed sticks into a pale blue diamond-shaped kite. Following his directions, I walked it a dozen or more steps away and held it up; then he twitched it from my hands. It caught the breeze and soared, sweeping up like a joyful soul going to its heavenly reward. "Good," Ben murmured. "Good, good. I will give you a slow count to fifty to hurry round to the far side. You know what to do then."

In the light of the crescent moon, which had dropped almost to the horizon, I could see the ghostly shape of the kite high above the house. I hurried around to my station— even from that side of the house, opposite to the parlor, I could hear Constable Potts snoring like a sawyer. In the shadows beneath a grove of bare-branched elms I waited, staring anxiously up at the fluttering shape in the sky. And then, suddenly, it plunged. Like a falling leaf it tumbled down, coming to earth not far from where I stood. I picked it up and felt where Ben had ripped away the second string, parting the silk and making the kite fall. As he had told me to do, I began to pull the kite string—a doubled string, really—steadily over the roof of the house.

Almost at once I felt resistance, as though a heavier weight had been tied to the string. I pulled for what felt like an hour, though in reality it could hardly have been three minutes. Then I held a cord in my hands, the one that Ben had attached to the end of the string. Three more minutes of hauling on this—and it, too, grew suddenly heavy—and I held in my hands the rope that Ben had tied to the cord. I looped it around the trunk of one of the elms and tied it good and fast.

Then I ran back. Ben stood on the ground just below Mrs. Worth's window. "All ready?" he asked.

"Yes! Don't make too much noise!"

"I have replaced my shoes with list slippers," he said. He began to climb the rope like a monkey, hand over hand. I could just make out his shape in the fading moonlight when he reached the window, and I heard him grunt as he wrapped the rope around his middle and tied it. Now he could keep one hand free. Slowly, oh so slowly, he silently worked the window sash open. Then, as he had done from the ladder, he pulled himself inside.

A moment later I felt the rope twitch. With my heart in my mouth, for I never liked high places, I tied the rope beneath my arms and gave two answering tugs. Then it was as if I were flying. Ben was pulling me up the side of the house.

As soon as I could, I grasped the sill and took some of my weight. Ben helped me through the window. He was panting. "No one would ever say you are a light girl, Patience," he whispered. I did not reply. "Light" girls are those who are vain, stupid, and wicked—or who weigh less than I. I did not care to ask precisely what Ben meant by the word.

"You are strong in the shoulders," I told him.

"That comes of carrying cases of lead type. And of swimming, no matter what James says of the sport."

We caught our breaths for a short time. From downstairs came the steady buzz of the constable's snoring. At last Ben closed the curtains and took a tinderbox from his pocket. He struck a spark, got a little flame going, and in the light of that he found Mrs. Worth's bedside candlestick. It was empty.

"We should have brought a candle!" Ben said.

"I know where she kept them." It was an odd place, a tall brass cylinder that had once been a map case. Her husband had brought it home after one of his voyages. I felt down in it and took out one of the dozen or so candles that remained. Ben struck another flame, and I held the wick in it until it caught with a little puff of white smoke. Then I put the new candle into the holder.

"Beeswax," Ben said. "Very nice."

I had forgotten that he had once been apprenticed to a chandler. "Give it to me," I said, and I set the candlestick on the floor and raised the bedclothes.

Sure enough, there was no box beneath the bed. Ben must have been right about the Worth men having searched there.

"This is where she usually put it. What could have happened to it?" I asked Ben.

"I don't know. Unless one of the constables stole it, or unless Mrs. Worth found a better hiding place."

I prowled around as quietly as I could, looking everywhere in case Mrs. Worth had somehow taken it into her head to hide the box elsewhere. It was not in her dresser, nor on top of it, nor behind it, not in the closet, or on the shelves, or in any drawer of her little writing desk, or under the covers, or between mattress and springs.

Ben, who had been helping me search, suddenly said, "Smell that."

I sniffed. There was a kind of pungent odor. "It's where Mrs. Worth vomited, maybe," I whispered back.

"Aye, I'd forgotten that. Well, well. Shall we look elsewhere?

"I don't think she even got out of bed, much less out of the room," I told Ben. "She had the box out just before she went to bed. She would have slipped it back beneath the bed before retiring. If she had risen and walked about during the night, I should have heard her. I sleep more lightly than the constable downstairs, and the bedroom floor and the door both creak terribly unless you tread lightly, as we have been doing. If she didn't put the strongbox back in its place beneath her bed, I can't think what she would have done with it, unless she went mad and threw it out the window!"

"'Tis a pretty puzzle," Ben muttered. "How could the box vanish from a sealed room?" Then he said, "Aha!" and went in triumph to the fireplace.

It was clean—Mrs. Worth had it lit only on the very coldest evenings of the year, and it had not held a fire all summer—so there was no ash beneath which the box might have been hidden. But the chimney—I had not thought of the chimney.

Setting the candle inside the fireplace, Ben got on hands and knees and inspected. The flue was open. He rolled up his sleeve and thrust his hand up, feeling around. He made a sour face. "Nothing here," he said.

His arm came away black with soot, though.

"I need something to get a little of this off," Ben told me.

I tore the hem of my petticoat, and he scrubbed the soot

as well as he could. "I don' t think we should leave anything behind," he said, balling up the cloth, cleanest side out, and stuffing it into his pocket. With an irritable sigh he added, "We'd better leave. It's at least one o'clock, and I dare not press our luck much further."

He lowered me from the window, making me feel giddy, and then he climbed down himself. We went round the house and untied the rope from the tree. "I couldn't let the window all the way down from the outside," he said to me. "I hope no one will notice." We bundled everything up, as neatly as we could, and started back to Queen Street.

We got back to the printing shop without incident. The clocks had just struck half past one. "Will you be able to sneak back into your house tonight?" I asked Ben.

"I have been in and out more often than my father would believe possible," he assured me. He sighed. "I'm sorry we didn't find the strongbox."

"So am I. Tomorrow we shall have to try and think of another plan."

He agreed, and we parted. This time, probably from mere nervous reaction, I fell asleep at once and did not awaken again until morning. When I did, my first thought was that I had caught cold, for my head ached and my eyes were runny. However, that was not enough to excuse me from a day's work. I rose, washed as well as I could in cold water, and when Ben showed up with some rolls and cheese, we ate hurriedly, Ben complaining that his arms and shoulders ached.

We barely managed our hasty breakfast before Mr. James showed up. I began my tasks, lighting the fire in the stove, dusting, and sweeping. Ben and Mr. James began to operate the press, and page upon page of the *Courant* began to issue out, with Ben and one other boy running back and forth to hang them on the rack so the ink could dry, or taking down and folding the dried sheets.

I felt unwell for all that morning, and at first I blamed the cheese, thinking it must have been spoiled. But then it began to occur to me that my symptoms—watery eyes, upset stomach, headache—were close to those of Mrs. Worth. How could I have been poisoned, though? I sternly told myself that it was all in my imagination—but then a pale-faced Ben, working away at the press lever, suddenly dashed across the room to a waste pail, bent double, and vomited violently.

"What ails you?" James yelled at him angrily, as if puking were a kind of boy's sport. "Finish that and get back to work!"

"I'm sick!" Ben gasped.

"I'll make you sicker!"

"No," Ben pleaded as James grabbed him by the back of his shirt and turned him around. "Don't shake me, James, please don't—"

"You can't be sick today!" James shouted. "Not with the paper to get out!"

"Please, sir," I said, "I will work the press. Let Ben rest."

"There, you see?" James said in a nasty tone. "A mere girl shames you! I will give you one half hour to feel better, Ben."

Ben nodded miserably and sank into one of the chairs, staying close to the pail. Mr. James showed me how to pull the great lever so the press would work. First he inked the type, and then he placed a sheet of paper in the frame, and when I pulled the lever hard, the press came down and the frame slid under it, so the type imprinted the blank paper. Then I pushed the lever the other way, the frame slipped back out, and Mr. James took off the printed sheet and replaced it with a blank one. No wonder Ben had such prodigious strength in his arms and shoulders! After but six or eight sheets I was gasping for breath.

Still, it was interesting to do something I had never before done, and I put all my attention into it. That was why I did not notice the man who came into the shop. Not until a dreadfully familiar voice said, "James Franklin! Is the

Courant so desperate for help that you put Quaker girls to work?"

Despite myself I looked around in quick fear.

The man cried out in astonishment, "Patience Martin!"

Mr. David Worth had recognized me.

Eleven

A good man is seldom uneasy, an ill one never easy.
—*Poor Richard's Almanac*

I suppose that of all the bad luck that showered down upon me that morning, the only particle of good was the fact that the constable who came when one was sent for was Mr. Wilkes, who did not manhandle me or shout in my face. I stood with my eyes downcast, mutely shaking my head at all of Mr. David's questions, refusing to answer him. When Mr. James began to upbraid me for my lies, my impertinence, and my deceptions, Ben immediately sprang to my defense: "Brother, I—"

"Ben did not know the truth," I said all in a rush, speaking for the first time since Mr. David had shouted my name. Ben fell silent, giving me a pleading look, but to save his hide I went on. "I needed a place to stay, and I persuaded him that I was Mercy Dyer, and he took pity on me and found the job for me, that is all."

Mr. James clouted Ben on the back of the head anyway. "Cleaning girl!" he exclaimed. "From now on you shall have the cleaning duties on top of your other work! Maybe if I pile chore on chore I can find some way to weary you to the point of not landing yourself and me in such trouble!"

"Patience Martin," said the constable, "I apprehend you in the King's name on a charge of breaking the terms of your indentures. You must come with me to stand before the magistrate and be charged."

I tried to signal Ben to keep still and not speak of how he had helped me, but I had no way of knowing whether he understood me or not. Before a good half hour had passed, Constable Wilkes had hauled me before a man named Mr. Thomas, a lean-cheeked old white-haired man who from his spot on the judge's bench peered at me through heavy black-rimmed spectacles. "And what is this wench here for?" he asked in a piping voice. "What is the charge?"

Constable Wilkes reeled off the story: I had run from my lawful indenture, had taken a false name, and had deceived Mr. James Franklin into hiring me and paying wages, when my labor was owed to my legal master. Somewhat to my surprise the old judge gave a snort at that, and his icy old face thawed into a kind of nasty smile. "Then that at least is money he will not recover, the rogue," he observed. "The *Courant* prints nothing but vicious lies, and those by the bushel measure! Is there anyone here to speak for the girl?"

"Yes, Your Honor," said Mr. David, stepping forward. "My father holds her indentures, inherited from my aunt, the late Mrs. Abedela Worth, waiting only for the reading of the will. If Your Honor please, I will stand bond for the girl and put up her surety."

"Then I bind her over into the hands of Mr. David Worth," the judge said. "Let us say a bond of, oh, only a pound, because she caused some trouble to that pestiferous printer Franklin."

Mr. David took out a purse and counted out notes and coins until he had made up the sum. There was some little business of writing up a document, signing and sealing it, and then I found myself in the street, with Mr. David holding my arm above the elbow and steering me down toward Orange Street. "Patience," he said in a not unkind voice, "you did very wrong to run."

"I know that is how you see it, sir," I answered dully. "Only please understand why I ran away. Your father said he was ready to sell me to anyone, for any kind of labor at all, and that he hoped my new master would be harsh. Very well,

I can stand harsh treatment, but I cannot abide the thought of being made nothing better than a mere slave."

"I remember your mother," he said thoughtfully. "Although I met her but twice, I think. She died of smallpox, did she not?"

"Yes, sir," I said. "In the last epidemic before this past summer's."

"And your father, Adam Martin, was my uncle's first mate aboard the brig *Swiftsure*. I remember him, too, a tall, brawny Englishman from Portsmouth, not a man to take an insult lightly or to stand much abridgement of his liberties. I believe I understand where your stubbornness comes from." He sighed. "My father is not a well man. The doctor says he has eaten some poison. My father says no, it is some dire spell cast by the witch Moll Bacon—"

"She is not a witch!" When he looked at me in surprise, I added, "I do not believe in witches or magic, sir."

He shook his head as if I had said something foolish. "No? I have met many thoughtful and intelligent men, both here and in England, who would disagree with you, girl. I don't know, I confess, just what I think myself. In the light of day such things as witches seem absurd, I grant you. But in the deep of night, with the branches of the trees scraping against the walls of the house in the wind, and a dismal howling coming from the gusts in the chimney, why then I'm apt to believe that Old Splitfoot himself is prowling about, seeking souls to seize."

We arrived at the Worths' house, and he paused. "Listen, Patience. Try to be like your name for a change, and show some of that virtue in dealing with Father. I will speak to him—though I declare he holds me in nearly the same contempt as he holds you—and will try to abate his anger. He is still keeping to his bed, and I think it probable that for a day or two at least you will not have to face him. But you must give me your word, your sacred word, not to run away again, or I cannot help you."

"Yes, sir," I said.

"Do you give your word?"

I swallowed hard. "I give my word, sir."

We went in, and he sent me straight to the kitchen, where the thin, worried-looking Betty Thayer hugged me and wept over me. She exclaimed in surprise at my clothing: "Why, where are your own dresses?" she asked. "You look quite different in those Quaker garments!"

"I traded my own clothes for these," I said, thinking that was not really a lie, or at least not much of one, for I had exchanged wearing my own dresses for the two Ben had brought me.

"Never mind, never mind," she said, putting her head to one side as she looked at me very closely. "I have some dresses of my daughter Eliza's left from when she was about your age. They will need some taking up, for she was a larger girl than you then—you would not think so to see her today, would you, but then I suppose you have not seen Eliza, for she has worked so hard these seven years past for a strict gentleman in Marblehead—oh, never mind. I will try the dresses on you, and we will ply our needles as we must to make them fit. They are nearly ten years old, but you will not mind that, I'm sure." She smiled at me. "I'm so happy to see you safe and whole, Patience. I imagined the most terrible things when you went away."

Betty's obvious feelings touched my heart, for in my life there had been very few people who would have given me a second thought, let alone who would have been glad to see me after an absence. She brought three dresses, plain but decent, and I tried them on. All were too large in the waist and shoulders, and too long by three inches. Betty fed me and then afterward set me in a corner of the kitchen with scissors and needle and thread, and I began to alter the dresses to fit me.

I was still there when Betty came in from the front of the house with a newspaper. "The boy selling these asked me to give this to you," she said, offering it to me. "Don't let Mr. Richard know, for the *Courant* vexes him so!"

Ben. The newsboy must have been him. I took the paper from Betty and skimmed through it. Most of it I had already seen—the attack on inoculation and on Cotton Mather, the list of shipping news, and all the rest—but in the bottom right-hand corner of the front page, a little paragraph had been squeezed in. I read it, wondering what on earth had possessed Ben to write it, for it bore the earmarks of his style of talking:

> The Wise say, "put first things first, and the rest must follow." Patience Martin, a runaway bond servant sought in Connexion with the Death of Mrs. Abedela Worth, has been taken by Mr. Josiah Wilkes of the Boston Constabulary. Benjamin Franklin, apprentice at the *Courant*, learn'd that she hath been Released on Bond to Mr. David Worth, the Son of her lawful Master. Comes next Week, she must be Arraigned and Question'd of certain Matters regarding the Death of Mrs. Worth, which was Last Week reported in these Pages. Tonight the girl lodges at the Home of Mr.

THE SECRET OF THE SEALED ROOM

Richard Worth, in Orange Street near Boston
Neck where it Becomes the Roxbury Road
The. Midnight death of Mrs. Worth still hath
Baffl'd the Authorities.

I wondered that they had been able to work that story
into the newspaper at all. It must have been set into type
at the very last minute, and I imagined that to make room
for it there, Ben must have had to reset the whole front
page, and the papers had all to be printed afresh. Indeed,
it looked very like it had been done in haste, for there was
a bad error near the end. "The" obviously belonged with
"Midnight," but there it was, set off with a period, in the
wrong place.

Yet . . . how came that to be, with such a hand as Ben's
setting up the type? How could he possibly have made
such a glaring mistake? I had seen his quick and steady
skill at setting type, and this was not like him. And as far
as that went, why did he start the little article with that
silly, useless quotation? I did not see how the supposed
sentiment of the Wise had any bearing on my situation or
on the news story.

The moment I had been most dreading came in late
afternoon, when Betty told me that I was to take Mr.

Richard's dinner to him on a tray. It was not a plentiful meal: a bit of baked codfish, a relish of chopped cabbage and onions with a vinegar sauce, a few small boiled potatoes, and a half mug of small beer. I hated facing the man, and the tray trembled in my hands, but I ascended the stair without spilling anything, and as his bedroom door stood open, I paused there, did a sort of awkward dip in place of a curtsey, and said, "I have your dinner, sir," in a not-very-confident voice.

"Bring it to me," he said, leaning back on a pile of pillows and glaring at me with no good expression.

He looked quite ill, his eyes rimmed with red, his cheeks pale, but he also looked very angry. I timidly carried the tray to where he sat propped in bed and placed it on his lap for him. "You have much abused my trust and patience, you saucy young wench," he said harshly, his feverish eyes snapping in irritation. "I hope you have prayed to ask the Lord for forgiveness!"

I stared at the tray and said nothing, for I was afraid that once I began to speak, I should lose all control of my tongue and it would land me in worse trouble yet. "Here I have taken you into my own house," he went on. "You have eaten my food and slept under my roof, and you reward me by running away! What were you about, you wretched girl?"

"Sir," I said softly, "I ran from here because I did not wish to be bought and sold, like an animal."

"You are a bond servant," he chided me, as though I really needed to be reminded of that hateful fact. "You have no rights to claim, and no say in the matter. I shall have to be most careful in choosing a new master for you, you ungrateful little wretch—I will bind you to someone who does not believe in sparing the rod, nor in spoiling the child!"

I could feel the nails of my clenched fingers stabbing into the flesh of my palms. Telling myself that I must not, that I would not, answer back, I simply stared at the tray, feeling my cheeks burning hot.

Then Mr. Richard's voice took on a new tone, still grinding but oddly sweet, like honey poured over rusty gears: "However, if you are sorry for your ill behavior and show your repentance by returning my sister-in-law's iron money box to me, I could change my mind."

I shook my head. "I don't know where it is, sir."

"You do know the strongbox I speak of, though? You have seen it?"

"Yes, sir, often. Mrs. Worth had it in her room that last night, but since then I haven't seen it again."

"Perhaps that wicked Moll Bacon slipped it into her basket before she left."

"No, sir, she couldn't have. I saw the strongbox in Mrs. Worth's hands long after Moll left the house."

"Lies and more lies!" With an irritable snarl he picked up the fork and cut a small bite from the codfish. "Eat this," he said, holding it out toward me.

"Sir?"

Roughly, Mr. Richard growled, "The fool of a doctor thinks I was poisoned! Very well, from now until I find a place for you that will get you permanently off my hands, you shall taste my food before I eat it, and if it is poisoning me, so shall it you. Eat this!"

And so I nibbled the bite of baked fish, then sampled the cabbage and onion dish and a bit of the potatoes. He made me take a sip of the beer, too, which disgusted me with its foul taste, and then as he began to eat, he brusquely told me I could go.

As I turned, he lashed me with the most hateful words yet: "You will have your freedom in only four years, and that is far too good for you! If I can possibly manage it so, those shall be the longest and hardest four years of your life! By rights you should be returned to Charleston and restored to the man who was robbed of your worthless mother!"

I stopped momentarily in my tracks, my heart thumping so hard it was a wonder he could not hear its pounding. "Do not revile my mother, sir," I said, but very softly.

"Eh? Eh? Do you talk back to me, you saucy young hussy?"

Instead of looking back at him, which would only make me angrier, I simply shook my head and left with what little dignity I could muster, my eyes stinging. But I held in my tears somehow.

That evening, strange though it seems, I began to sorely miss my cramped little sleeping booth in the printing house. There at least I had a kind of private room to myself. Here I had to lie in a corner of the kitchen, with no candle and no books for company. Worse, Betty Thayer had been told to shackle me, to lock an iron cuff to my ankle and to chain that to a leg of the stove. She was weeping hard when she came in with the rattling chain and the cuff. I saw at once what she was about, and I told her, "Don't cry. I know this is not your fault."

"I would not keep a dog on a chain," she said bitterly. She knelt, I put forth my leg, and she sprang back up again, throwing the iron cuff to the floor with a bang. "I won't do it! God forbid that I treat you so, and you hardly more than a child!"

"I won't run away," I promised her. "Thank you for your kindness in not chaining me."

"Don't tell Mr. Richard that I didn't, or I'll feel his anger too," she said.

"I would never tell him such a thing. Thank you, Betty."

She bent to kiss me on the forehead. "Will you be warm enough, dear? I will bring you extra blankets if you wish."

"No, thank you. The stove has left the kitchen quite warm. Only may I have a candle, please, and something to read? It helps me to sleep."

The candle was no trouble, and she brought me a smelly little tallow dip in a moment. As for books, she said the only ones in the house were up in Mr. Richard's room, but she did give me the *Courant,* which she and the other servants had now scanned through.

It was hardly entertaining, and I had read almost all of it already, but I lay back and in the yellow glow of the tallow candle went through it all again, pausing at the paragraph Ben himself must have put in about my being taken. I still thought it read oddly. As I said, Ben was far too good a compositor to have made such a ridiculous mistake as placing that period on the wrong side of "The."

Then suddenly I leaned up on my elbow, my eyes wide as I stared at the error. The flickering yellow light showed me something I had not seen before: a whole different meaning, with the clue in the first sentence. "Put first things first, and the rest must follow" indeed!

It was a clever hint. Taking it, I read just the *first* words from the following sentences: *Patience. Benjamin. Comes. Tonight. Midnight.*

The misprinted news item was Ben's way of getting a secret message to me, a message telling me that he was coming to visit. I looked at the hall clock and saw that the time was already past nine. I wondered what young Ben had in mind, and what further trouble it would bring. Well, I would not have to wait very long to find out.

❧ Twelve ❧

I . . . spent but little upon myself except . . . in books.
—*The Autobiography of Benjamin Franklin*

I dozed fitfully, wrapped in my blanket but fully dressed, for the first couple of hours. Then I lay wide awake to hear the town clocks strike eleven, the quarter hour, the half hour, the three quarters . . . and it seemed an eternity before at last a deep, solemn midnight struck. I rose before the first three chimes had sounded, and I tiptoed to the kitchen door, quietly opened it, and looked out. The night was cool but clear, and the waxing moon silvered the yard. I saw no Ben Franklin. I decided to wait there for him until I could count slowly to five hundred, and I stood with the door cracked just wide enough for me to peer out into the night.

I had arrived at three hundred and forty-one when I saw a dark figure slipping across the lawn, stepping fast. My first thought was to call out to him quietly and then step out onto the small back porch, but I did not want to make even that much noise, for Mr. Richard's bedroom was almost directly above the kitchen, and Betty had told me that when his stomach distressed him, he would lie wakeful through much of the night.

A moment later I felt glad that I had not called out, for as the person came to the front steps, I saw it was not Ben at all, but Mr. David. It was cool enough so that I could see his breath condensing as he drew near. He went up the front steps, and I heard the very faint sound of the front door being carefully opened. Alarmed, I hastily closed the back door, as noiselessly as ever I could, and dived back into my pallet bed. I closed the shackle over my left ankle, hoping that it would stay there without a lock if I had to get up and walk. Then I pulled the blankets over me and wrapped myself tight inside them like a caterpillar snug in a cocoon.

A moment later Mr. David stepped into the kitchen. He was holding a lighted candle and moved so silently that I knew he had slipped off his shoes. He paused in the doorway as if studying my stretched-out figure, and then in a soft voice he whispered, "Patience?"

Though my heart was hammering hard, I lay still and pretended to be asleep. He set the candle on the table and fell a-rummaging in the pantry. I thought he might have taken too much wine, from the unsteady sounds he made— not loud, but random and haphazard. When he knocked something small over, I could not well go on pretending sleep, so in a dazed voice I asked, "Who is there?"

"It's I," he said in his curious accent, half Boston, half British, and his words were slurred. "I didn't mean to wake you, Patience. I was hungry, so I came down to see if there might be something to eat."

"There is part of the custard pie," I said. "And I think there may be a cold chicken's leg. Shall I get up, sir, and find you something? You will have to step out until I have dressed."

More rattling sounds. "No, no, don't trouble yourself, Patience. I have them. Go on sleeping, and don't mind me."

I lay in an agony of suspense, hoping that Ben would spy the candlelight in the kitchen window and have the sense not to come boldly up and tap on the door. Mr. David made up a plate of food, bade me a soft good night, and left. I sprang up as soon as he was gone, unsnapped the shackle, and went to listen at the kitchen door. Away in the house I heard the steps creak very softly as he took his late meal upstairs to his room. When all seemed safe, I opened the back door again and nearly cried out, for standing on the back porch and facing me was Ben, so near I could touch him.

"Shh!" he said, unnecessarily. Then all in a rush, but in a whisper, he went on: "I saw Mr. Worth come inside and thought it best to wait outside until I was sure he was out of the way."

"Come in," I said. "Be quiet, whatever you do!"

Ben stepped just inside, and I closed the door. "This feels good," he said, for the stove still gave out some warmth. "I have been sick all afternoon and only now feel some better. Are you recovered?"

"I feel quite well again," I told him."My headache is gone."

"And I at least kept my dinner down. Do you have any idea what happened, why we grew so ill?"

"Not I."

"Patience," he said, "while we were in Mrs. Worth's house, we were poisoned!"

"How could that be?" I asked. "Neither of us ate or drank anything at all while we were there!"

"That is the cleverness of the murderer at work! I knew that once I had read something that put me in mind of Mrs. Worth's strange mode of death, and at last I remembered it. Here, take this."

In the darkness I could not see what he was offering me, but he thrust something hard against my stomach. I took it: a book of some kind, a small octavo book, only about six by nine inches, but heavyish. "What have you found?"

"'Tis a volume crammed full with true tales of murders and murderers," Ben said. "I read it some time back, and when I was trying to think of what might have poisoned us, I recollected a story in it. 'Tis told in chapter seventeen. I think that the same trick that chapter describes is what killed Mrs. Worth—and what made us sick!"

Clutching the book, I told him, "I dare not light a candle. Mr. David is still awake upstairs. If he should bring his dirty dishes back down, he would see the light for certain."

"Then I'll tell you," said Ben, keeping his voice to a whisper. "I just read it afresh this evening, so I have all the facts yet clear in memory. It is a story of King Leopold of Hungary. Listen!"

There in the dark Ben breathlessly spun out the tale, keeping his voice low. In the year 1671, Leopold, who was not only the king of Hungary but the Holy Roman Emperor to boot, grew seriously ill with symptoms of racking headaches, vomiting, and terrible stomach cramps. It was apparent to all, Ben said, that Leopold was gravely ill, on the very edge of death, and no doctor seemed able to offer him help or hope. In his distress the ailing monarch consulted with an Italian alchemist, Francesco Borri. A physician as well as a supposed practitioner of magic arts, Borri was at that time a prisoner, wanted by the Catholic Inquisition, but the king offered the man sanctuary and promised him his freedom if he could find a cure.

Borri, Ben said, soon enough suspected a slow poisoning by arsenic, but for some weeks he could find no means by which the king could have been swallowing the poison. There was certainly no poison in the king's food and drink, and yet he was clearly being slowly killed by arsenic poisoning. Borri tried and tried to understand the odd case but had no success for a long time.

Then one night when he was called in because Leopold was suffering horrible pangs, Borri noticed that the air in the ailing king's bedroom seemed unusually thick and oppressive—it had an ill smell that the king had become accustomed to and so no longer noticed. The alchemist immediately realized that something had befouled the very atmosphere of the room. Borri took several of the king's candles and very precisely weighed them against exactly the same kind of candles taken from elsewhere in the same building, and he found that the king's candles were all just the tiniest bit heavier.

From this Borri concluded that the wicks of Leopold's candles had been soaked in a solution of arsenic, and that night after night the poison fumes filled the very air he breathed, slowly ruining his health and threatening his life.

With this knowledge Leopold was saved, and eventually he recovered completely and went on to rule for another thirty-five years. Unfortunately, concluded Ben, the discovery did poor Borri no good at all. He told me, "The poisoners were renegade Jesuits, and to placate them, Leopold became a Jesuit too—and then, despite his first promise, he sent Borri right back to prison! Never trust the benevolence of kings—"

I interrupted him: "Poisoned candles?" I blinked in the darkness. "And when we were in Mrs. Worth's bedroom last night, you lit one of her beeswax candles so we could see to search for the strongbox! We breathed the air in that room for the best part of an hour! But how could we prove the candles were poisoned, Ben? Oxen and wain-ropes could not drag me back inside Mrs. Worth's house—"

"We don't need to go back there," Ben assured me. "Last night I did not want to leave a partly burned candle behind as a clue that someone had been slipping around in there—and so before I climbed out the window, I pocketed the one that we used. I still have that candle, and I've taken part of it to Dr. Blackthorn already to see if he can test it for arsenic."

"Part of it?"

"Aye," said Ben. "I cut it in half and kept the bottom. The stub end of it had a mark, a little bas-relief figure of a bee, showing that it had come from a mold, and there was an imperfection. The left half of the bee was a few hairs-breadths misaligned with the right. I have kept that part of the candle to use as a comparison. If we find the mold with just that flaw in the figure of the bee, we will know for certain who made those candles!"

I was frowning in the dark, my spirits sinking, and I felt a gloomy sort of pleasure in knowing that Ben could not see my face, for I am sure it must have been a mask of dismay.

However, though I held my tongue, he seemed to guess that something had upset me, for he asked me, "What's the matter?" He had a quick mind, for without waiting for an answer he jumped to the correct conclusion immediately: "You already know who poisoned those candles!"

"Not exactly. I do know where they came from," I said unwillingly.

Ben's whisper took on an agitated, urgent edge: "Don't make me draw it out of you a crumb at a time, like the meat picked from a cracked black walnut! Who gave them to her?"

"Mr. David brought them to the house," I said in a miserable voice. "He gave three dozen beeswax candles to me and said that Betty Thayer had made more than he and his father could use, and that Mrs. Worth might as well have the rest."

"Betty Thayer, Mr. Worth's cook," Ben said after me. "But that makes no sense. Why would she wish to poison Mrs. Worth? Had she any reason to hate her?"

"I don't know." But though I wished to say nothing to get the woman in trouble, I was guessing wildly. I knew very well that Betty had small love for any Worth: Mr. David she tolerated, barely, though she deplored his unsteady nature and often complained to me about his aptness to fall in with wild young companions at Harvard, as 'twas rumored he had done whilst in college in England. Mr. Richard she viewed with distaste, resentment, and dread, for he was a hard and overbearing master and quick to complain.

As for Mrs. Worth—well, I knew of no real quarrel between them, but Mrs. Abedela Worth, like her brother-in-law Mr. Richard, had an acid, scolding tongue and an irritable disposition to match. It was quite easy for me to imagine Mrs. Worth upbraiding her brother-in-law's cook for any little slight or error, either real or fancied. Mrs. Worth had often enough given me a slap across the face for something I had not even done, and never once had she apologized upon learning her mistake. Still, I had borne these injuries, and never once had I thought of killing my mistress, or even of wishing her dead, and I could believe no such ill nature resided in Betty Thayer, who had treated me kindly. "She would have to be mad to poison Mrs. Worth," I told Ben.

"Mrs. Thayer might have made the poisoned candles for Mr. Worth. Maybe she didn't know that he would give some of them to his sister-in-law."

I had not thought of that. "It was unusual for him to give anything away," I reluctantly agreed.

The clocks struck the three-quarter hour, and Ben said, "I have to go. Read the book, chapter seventeen, and see what it says about deadly candles and how they affect their victims. I will get word to you somehow of what the doctor learns about the candle. We don't even know for certain yet whether the thing is poisoned. But if Dr. Blackthorn finds that the wick contains arsenic—well, in that case, things may not look too good for Betty Thayer."

Or for me, he might have added. Here I had been thinking Betty the only friend I had in the Worth household. Without her I was down to only one person in the world who cared enough about me to offer help—and he was a printer's apprentice who spent most of his own life in trouble.

But what if Ben was wrong, and Mrs. Worth *had been* meant to have the poisoned candles? Might not someone else have given Mrs. Thayer a coil of poisoned candlewick with which to mold the fine beeswax candles? Someone who would profit from Mrs. Worth's death—like her brother-in-law, Mr. Richard? My head whirled round and round with doubts and suspicions that I could not resolve or prove.

I crept back into bed, hiding the book beneath the folded blanket I used as a pillow, but for the rest of that night I slept very little.

Thirteen

Don't misinform your doctor.
—*Poor Richard's Almanac*

The whole household was thrown into considerable confusion the next morning, for Mr. Richard, although still feeling unwell, insisted he had to be about his business and rose with the sun. Mrs. Thayer, roused from sleep to prepare his breakfast, first begged my forgiveness and then chained the hateful shackle to my ankle and to the stove.

When Mr. Richard came downstairs, leaning heavily on a stick, she humbly asked him if she might set me free from the chain, and he said shortly, "Aye, but I hold you responsible for her, so keep your eye on her this day. Let her help you. Give her the tasks you most dislike."

We made him a dish of minced potatoes, cheese, and onions, poured in three beaten eggs, and baked it. He complained of immoderate thirst, and Betty brewed him strong tea. Before he would take it, though, he forced me to drink about half a gill to make sure it was not poisoned. It was too strong for me, and my stomach heaved, but I got the liquid down. Mr. Richard also made me taste his breakfast, which was more grateful to my stomach than his, for he got only a few bites of it down before pronouncing himself without appetite. He did not feel up to the long walk into town, and so he sent the garden boy for two stout men and a sedan chair. Mr. Richard complained at the expense but climbed into the box, and the two bearers picked it up by the long handles, one man grasping the two in front, the other the two in the rear, and they set off down Orange Street toward town at a brisk enough pace.

Mr. David came downstairs some little time later and finished the rest of the breakfast dish Betty had cooked, then told her he would not be home for midday dinner, and he rode away on a chestnut mare. Betty and a younger woman who came in every few days, cleaned the house and set me to washing bed linens in the yard, hauling buckets of water from the well to the big iron washing cauldron, under which burned a pungent fire of pine and oak logs.

Washing is always hard work, and it is much harder when it must be done for a whole household and not just one person. I stirred the sheets around and around in the boiling, soapy water with a long pole, then hauled them out, heavy with the steaming water, and dumped them into a second cauldron to rinse them. I was more than happy when Betty came out and gave me a hand as I hung them to dry, for by then my shoulders ached.

In the early afternoon Ben Franklin came down Orange Street with copies of the *Courant* folded over his arm, and he found occasion to have a quick word with me: "Have you read the book?"

"No time. What says Dr. Blackthorn?"

"The candle was definitely filled with poison," he said shortly. "But I have told him it remains to see who put the arsenic into the wicks, and he has agreed to allow us a day or so to try to learn who might have done the deed."

At that point I heard Betty calling my name, and Ben said, "You'd better go. I will be back this way in an hour or so—see me then if you can."

Betty needed some help in turning the master's mattress, and we quickly finished the chore. Then she told me I might have a few minutes to rest, as both the Worth men were out of the house until late in the afternoon. I went to the kitchen and took the book from the folded blankets that had made up my pallet. I sat on them, with my back pressed into the corner, and opened the heavy little book to find chapter seventeen and read about the unfortunate Mr. Borri and the poisoned king. The title of the book was given on the cover as *Celebrated Murders and Capital Crimes, in England and Abroad,* by Michael Fortham, Gentleman. The volume had been much damaged by a soaking in water, and it was all warped and malformed. Still, it looked readable, and thinking that it sounded more interesting than *The Pilgrim's Progress,* but perhaps not so adventurous as *Robinson Crusoe,* I opened the book, and my eye chanced to fall on the title page and on the scribbled name of, I presumed, a former owner of the volume.

The signature was in a florid sort of script, with looping underlines, in an old-fashioned manner. The writing was clear to read, however: *Nathaniel Thayer.*

I felt chilled. Nathaniel was Betty Thayer's husband's name. And if the book had once belonged to him, then Betty could have read it. I did not want her to be the poisoner. Swallowing my fears, I found and read chapter seventeen and learned that I might as well have taken Ben's word for what it contained, since he had given an admirable summary of everything it told.

A few minutes later I volunteered to beat the entry-hall rug for Betty. That got me outside, and when Ben returned

(I saw he had sold all of his papers), he came to the far side of the carpet so we could converse without his being seen from the house at all. I had brought the book out with me, wrapped in the copy of the *Courant* that had contained Ben's message to me.

As soon as he arrived, I asked Ben where he had found the book. "Oh, 'tis mine. I bought it for a halfpenny," he said. "My friend Cooper works in a shop where they buy and sell used books. He knows how I love to read. This book had been lying unsold in the shop for some years. It's badly water damaged, and no one would buy it, but he thought it was one I might like, so he set it aside for me and let me have it cheap."

"Look at the first page," I told him. I put the wrapped book on the ground and began swinging my rod and bringing clouds of dust from the hanging carpet with each whack.

He stooped, then picked up and unwrapped the book. "Nathaniel Thayer," he said. "So? That's probably the original owner of the book."

"That is also the husband of Betty Thayer, Mr. Richard's cook," I said.

Ben whistled. "That means—"

"I know what it means. Ben, can you ask your friend Cooper whether he recalls who sold this book to his master?"

"Easily done," Ben said. "We shall have to act quickly, though. Dr. Blackthorn says he must go to the authorities within a day or so if we have no luck in learning who poisoned the candles." He took the book from me and ran off. I thought how seldom I had seen him walk like a Christian—his normal mode of moving, it seemed to me, was to run as if a fiend were on his heels.

Though I thought I was tolerably good at hiding my true feelings, having had much practice when working for the sharp-tempered Mrs. Worth, Betty asked me two or three times that afternoon if I was well. The truth was that I felt horribly sick, but not in body.

It also occurred to me that I might help Mr. Richard most by removing the candles from his bedroom. However, two things stopped me. First, I did not know whether all the candles in the house were from the same batch. Perhaps they all were poisoned—or all innocent! Second, and more important, I was afraid that Betty would have too many questions if she should catch me. All I could do, it seemed to me, was to try and discourage Mr. Worth from staying up late that evening.

I did slip upstairs, though, when Betty busied herself cooking supper for the Worth men, and I took one of the three candles in the holder on Mr. Worth's bedside table out to look at the base. Just as Ben had said, near the part of the candle that fit into the socket of the holder was the small, raised figure of a bee. And just as he had told me, the bee had a line or join down its middle, with the left side somewhat higher than the right. I had little doubt that this candle and the poisoned one had come from the same mold.

Dr. Blackthorn surprised us all by riding up in the early part of the evening. He swung off his gray mare, and Betty let him in. "Is my patient home yet?" he rumbled, taking off his hat as he stepped inside.

"No, sir. He would go to the office, despite all we could say."

The doctor sniffed the air. "Well, well, he's a headstrong fellow, Richard Worth. Have you roasted a chicken?"

"Yes, sir."

"Then I shall stay and have a bite with Richard. If he begrudges me a meal, I shall tell him it's either that or a half-crown doctor's fee!"

Betty chuckled at that, then covered her mouth with her fingers and scurried out. I curtseyed and turned to go, but the doctor said in a low voice, "Stay a moment, Patience."

"Yes, sir?"

"Ben has told me all about how you have tried to learn

the identity of our mystery poisoner. He thinks you are a very intelligent young woman, you know."

"No, sir, I didn't."

"Well, he does. And so do I. How close do you think you are?"

"Very close, sir," I said.

"Good. Now, here's what you are going to do: Run away from here."

"I cannot, sir," I said. "I gave my word to Mr. David."

"But you shall run away," he said firmly. "Go straight to the printing shop. Ben is there already. Now: Who shall I bring there?"

"Sir?"

"You are going to tell us all who poisoned Mrs. Abedela," the doctor told me. "Tonight. You must. I've arranged it all. Who must I bring to the shop?"

"Oh, sir," I said. "I don't know—"

"Make up your mind quickly."

I bit my lip. "If I must, sir, then you need to bring Mrs. Thayer. And both of the Worth gentlemen, for they should know how the poisoning has been done. But I do not know whether—"

"You shall have until eight o'clock tonight only. And if you have nothing to say, then I am afraid you will have to face Mr. Richard's wrath. I will protect you as far as I may. I'll even offer to buy your indentures, but I doubt Richard would part with them to me—he'd think I would be too soft on you. Go now. Run! As for your conscience, remember: It's doctor's orders!"

❦ Fourteen ❧

"We must all hang together."
—Benjamin Franklin at the signing
of the Declaration of Independence

I rushed into the print shop, panting for breath. Ben was there, with his brother James looming over him, looking furious. He whirled on me, and his red face grew even redder. "What next!" he exclaimed. "Mercy—Prudence—Patience—whatever your name is today, what the devil are you doing back here?"

"Dr. Blackthorn sent me, sir," I said.

"Dr. Blackthorn does not own this shop, mistress!" he snapped.

"James," said Ben pleadingly, "just think: If we can reveal the murderer here, in the office, you will have a story worth writing! Let us gather all those concerned here and let Patience point out the guilty one. Why, you will sell papers as they sell apples—by the bushel!"

I saw avarice and anger warring in the elder Franklin's face. Finally he threw his hands up in the air and said, "Oh, very well! Get out of my sight until they get here then! And stay out from underfoot!"

Ben and I retreated to the back room. "What did you find?" I asked. "About the book, I mean."

"The book? Oh! Cooper told me that when Nathaniel Thayer deserted her, his poor wife was left very destitute. As you know, she had just bound herself out to Mr. Richard Worth, but to make some money to buy herself and her daughter a few necessities, she sold all of her husband's possessions that she could. Among the rest she sent three or four baskets of his books over the course of several days to the shop to be sold for whatever money she could get. It must have come to the store in one of those, Cooper said. And since that book was warped by water, they cast it by, until one day Cooper asked me if I wanted to buy it—"

I wanted to shake him until his teeth rattled. "I understand, but that is not the important thing! Did she bring them to the shop herself?"

Ben threw up his hands in surrender. "Cooper did not know! He wasn't apprenticed in the shop then. His master, Mr. Athol, said he didn't recall, either."

I paced. "She sold the things after she had moved to Mr. Worth's house. I don't think she would have taken them herself to sell—she thought being deserted was a disgrace to her. Nor would she have sent her daughter, Eliza. Perhaps the garden boy—if Mr. Richard employed one back then. Or—" I shook my head. "'Tis all so tangled! It must come down to someone who had opportunity to read the book before bringing it to the shop for sale, someone who had opportunity—" I broke off. An idea had begun to glimmer somewhere in my mind—it was not clear, it was not within my grasp, but something was stirring.

"Do you—"

I raised my hand and shook my head. "Hush. I almost have it."

Though he could be so very talkative, Ben had the admirable gift of silence when it was most needed. He sat back, folded his arms, and waited whilst I thought. At last I said, "Aren't some of the young gentlemen who keep company here and chat so much students at Harvard?"

"Aye," said Ben. "There's Thomas Radcliffe and William Makepeace, for two."

I said, "Quick, bring me paper and pen."

Without asking why, Ben ducked into the shop, then returned with paper, pen, and ink. "I'll sharpen it for you," he said, taking out a penknife and working on the nib of the goose quill. He shaved it, blew on it, and said, "There, that should do."

"Which of those young men is closer?"

"Mr. Radcliffe," Ben said. "He does not lodge at Harvard, but toward Cornhill. . . ."

I was scribbling furiously, dipping the pen into the black ink and carefully forming the letters. I finished my brief note, blotted it carefully, and read through it. "Then could you run this to him—do not walk, run—and if he is not at home, could you find Mr. Makepeace instead?"

"That will be harder. I will have to cross the river to Cambridge. But I'll try Radcliffe first." He thrust the paper inside his shirt and dashed out. I heard James call irritably after him, but Ben did not tarry.

The clock struck six a moment later. I paced, worrying that I had an idea of what had happened, but no clear proof. If only there were some way to—yes, there was one. I went into the front of the office and said humbly, "Mr. Franklin, may I ask if Constable Wilkes is likely to be anywhere handy?"

"Aye," he said sourly. "I warrant you'll find him yonder at the prison."

That dreadful prison house again! I wished that I had

given Ben that errand and taken his as my own. But there was nothing else for it. I went out, crossed the street to the prison, and asked at the door for Constable Wilkes. The guard brought him to me. The constable spoke with me for ten minutes, expressed utter astonishment at my request, and then when I explained why I wanted what I asked for, he took me to the same magistrate who had heard my case, the elderly Mr. Thomas. "Tell him," Wilkes said.

I repeated my request. Judge Thomas raised his eyebrows. "And this has to do with Mrs. Worth's death?"

"It does, sir."

I could not read the expression on his lean, wrinkled face. "And these things are to be brought to that rascal Franklin's print shop?"

"Yes, your honor."

"And he does not like the idea at all?"

"He hates it, sir."

Mr. Thomas smiled, a quick expression on his ivory-white face like a crease suddenly appearing in a sheet of paper. "What are you waiting for, Mr. Wilkes? Send someone to fetch what the young lady asks for. And I think you and I will make two more at this party tonight at the print shop!"

Ben returned before anyone else had come. In a puzzled voice he said, "The answer, Mr. Radcliffe said, is, 'Yes, but now there are more.' More what? He kept the note!"

"Will he come?"

"He says he will."

And almost at that instant Constable Wilkes came into the shop, carrying a cylindrical brass map case. "Are these what you wanted?"

"Yes!" I said. I looked around. "Let's pull that small table here, and that one here, and put the chair between them. Like that, yes. Let me see." I reached into the case and pulled out candles. "There are nine left. Is there some place where we can find candles that look like these, as much alike as can be?"

"I know of some," Ben said. He snatched up one of the candles and tore out of the shop.

"I don't understand any of this," Constable Wilkes complained.

"Nor I," muttered James Franklin with a grunt.

Ben returned at twenty minutes to eight, with a dozen beeswax candles wrapped in a cloth. "These are close enough to any eye but a chandler's," he said. "Now what?"

We hurriedly took the old tallow candles out of their holders all round the shop and put in them eight of the fresh candles that Ben had brought. Four of these we put on the small table to the left of the chair, four to the right. The candles from Mrs. Worth's house, all but one, we replaced in the brass map cylinder.

Mr. Thomas Radcliffe, an uneasy-looking young man of college age, came into the shop, and Ben had him sit in a chair in the corner. And then the clock chimed eight, and pat on the hour a brace of horses drew up outside the shop. A moment later the door opened, and Mr. Richard Worth, leaning on a cane and breathing heavily, came in, with the doctor at his elbow. Mrs. Betty Thayer was just behind the doctor, and behind her came Mr. David Worth. And bringing up the rear was Judge Thomas, his face no longer unreadable. Indeed, he wore an almost impish expression of ill-concealed glee.

Mr. Richard stood glaring at me. "Arrest that girl," he croaked.

"She is under the eye of the law," said Judge Thomas with a smile. "I understand that she ran away from her indentures?"

"Twice!"

"Well, well, young Ben Franklin took her prisoner and has held her here, so the reward that you offered—"

"Reward!" shouted Mr. Worth.

"The reward you offered," continued Judge Thomas calmly, "should and must go to him."

"Why are we here?" asked Mr. David, cutting short his father's indignant spluttering.

"Why, we are here to learn what our young friends Patience and Benjamin have discovered about the death of Abedela Worth," Dr. Blackthorn told him. He held a chair. "Here, Richard, you will be more comfortable in this. Mrs. Thayer, here is a chair for you. Mr. Thomas, you must take this one—it is the most comfortable. Let us see: Constable Wilkes, you will probably want to stand. I will take this rather shabby armchair. Mr. David, you sit in the chair there, between the tables. Mr. Radcliffe is already settled comfortably in the corner. There, I think the rest of us can manage without chairs."

"Thank you, Doctor," said Ben grandly, stepping forward. "We will begin now. Patience will speak first."

All the gentlemen were staring at Ben as if he had quite lost his mind. "This is naught but a farce," snarled Mr. Richard. "Take that girl to a cell! I insist!"

"Not yet," said the judge. "In fact, we should have one last guest—ah, yes, here she is."

Mr. James stood very awkwardly beside the press, his face dark as a thunderstorm. He looked even angrier when a second constable pushed Moll Bacon into the shop.

"Prisoner," said the judge easily, "you shall stand there as though in the dock. Now, young people—astonish us!"

Fifteen

A kind of unprovoked murder . . .
—*The Autobiography of Benjamin Franklin*

And so we came to it at last, and I confess I stood with quaking heart. I had thought everything out so carefully—but what if I was wrong? What happened in the next half hour, I thought, would make or mar my life from here on.

I somehow gained control of my trembling voice and said, "Ben Franklin and I have learned a few things about how Mrs. Worth was poisoned. Let me tell you about them."

I spoke quickly of how we had sought the strongbox and had not found it, but I added that we had learned about another source of poison other than food and drink in Mrs. Worth's bedroom. "Both of us got somewhat ill from the poison. And Ben was clever enough to remember a book," I said. "One that spoke of such a poisoner's trick. We thought it possible that someone else had read that very story and, when the need arose, had remembered what was written there. Here is the book."

I held up the warped, water-damaged volume. Ben took it from me and said, "It would be too tedious for us all to take turns reading it. Here, Mr. David, you have been to college in England, and you have a good strong speaking voice. You shall read it aloud for us, if you please."

David Worth looked baffled, but he took the lumpish book from Ben. "Let me give you a light," Ben said, fetching a lit tallow candle and tipping one of the beeswax ones to light its wick. And then he repeated the action with a second, and a third, and kept on until all the eight candles on the tables were flaming.

"I don't need that much light," Mr. David protested.

"The print is dim, and the pages are water-stained," Ben said.

"Before you begin, sir," I said, "let us say first that the book used to belong to Mr. Nathaniel Thayer."

Betty gasped and clapped her hand to her mouth.

"His wife sold it when she was left alone to support their daughter," I continued.

"Read chapter seventeen, please, sir," said Ben.

Shaking his head, David Worth turned the pages, cleared

his throat, and started: "'Of a devilish device used in an attempt upon the life of Holy Roman Emperor Leopold, in the year 1671.'" He read until he mentioned the poisoned candles, and Ben said, "There, that is enough. You see? Candles that had their wicks soaked in an arsenic solution! Night after night Mrs. Worth read her Bible by the light of a candle that was slowly killing her."

"Candles that you brought to our house, Mr. David," I said.

"What?" David Worth smiled. "Patience, we had dozens of them! And we use the same candles in our house. There's nothing wrong with them."

"There is something else," I said. "On the morning that Mrs. Worth died, you sent Ben and me in search of your uncle. You remained behind. You could have taken the glass ball from the mantel. You could have then taken it to Moll Bacon's house to suggest she had done some evil magic. Did your father send you to inspect Moll's house, to search for the missing strongbox?"

"No," he said.

But immediately Mr. Richard growled, "Yes, I did!"

"I—I had not remembered that," Mr. David murmured. "Yes, I suppose I might have gone there."

"Then," I said, "you could have removed the glass ball

and hidden it where later the constables would find it—a way of throwing suspicion upon Moll."

Ben held up an unlit candle. "You would also have removed these had you found them before the constables came to secure the house," he said. "This is a telltale candle, you see." He showed everyone how the bee on the base was distinctive. "There were nine left," Ben said. "Exactly nine."

David Worth jerked his gaze down to the tables beside him. Four candles burned at his left elbow, four at his right. The ninth was in Ben's hand. With a convulsive gasp Mr. David started to rise.

"Nay," said Dr. Blackthorn, stepping forward and pressing his cane into Mr. David's chest, pinning him to the chair. "Let us study your symptoms, sir. Are you having difficulty breathing? Do you sweat, sir?"

Indeed, Mr. David's chest heaved, and his face shone with dripping perspiration.

"I sent Ben to ask one of the Harvard students about you, sir," I told the fear-stricken young man. "He learned that until lately you had large gambling debts. You paid some of them—the day after Mrs. Worth died. Is that not true, Mr. Radcliffe?"

"Thomas, please," groaned Mr. David with an anguished look at his friend.

Thomas Radcliffe would not meet his gaze. "It is true," he said in little more than a whisper. "God forgive you, David! You know it is true that you squared your debts the very day after your aunt's death. And you know full well that you have since run up even more. Just last night you stayed late at Wertham's, playing for reckless stakes, and lost heavily. You are not a lucky gambler, David."

"You young scoundrel," said Dr. Blackthorn in his rumbling voice. "You murdered your aunt, took the money from her strongbox, and paid your debts with that. But that money was not enough for you—and so you have started to use the poisoned candles on your father as well! He would inherit his sister-in-law's money, and when you had killed him, you would inherit both his and hers!"

"Please," croaked Mr. David.

"We will find the candle mold, you know," Constable Wilkes said.

Mr. David was writhing in his chair, his face an agony. He was sobbing bitterly by then. "Please."

I felt almost sorry for Mr. David, looking so hopeless and trapped. But he did not confess at once—not until his father, Mr. Richard, himself broke down into horrible, racking tears. Oddly, that somehow touched his soul, and Mr. David told us all at last. It was just as I had thought. He told about the poison, the candle mold, and even the strong-box, which he had forced open. He had thrown the empty box into the Mill Pond. Mr. David begged for forgiveness, which no one granted.

"Well," said Judge Thomas, standing. "It seems to me that a grave injustice has been done. Mistress Bacon, as soon as I may have the release order writ out, you will be free to go, and all charges against you will be dropped. Mr. Wilkes, apprehend this man on a charge of murder. Mr. Franklin—if I see one word of this in the *Courant*, sir, I shall clap you in prison!" To Ben and me he said, "Well done, young friends. Quite well done."

Ben bowed, quite gracefully, I thought, acknowledging the judge's kind words. I tried to put a smile on my face.

But inside I felt empty and sad.

Sixteen

Virtue and happiness are mother and daughter.
—*Poor Richard's Almanac*

The constables dragged Mr. David out, he pleading, protesting, and struggling the entire way. In his armchair Mr. Richard lay back, pale and perspiring, still gasping from his bitter bout of weeping. "My own son," he groaned. "I knew he was wild, but I never thought him capable of such a vile act as this. Never!"

Dr. Blackthorn took his pulse. "The law must deal with him as it may," he said solemnly. "But I will tell you this, sir: You have had the narrowest of escapes. I believe you will recover fully in time, but I tell you truly, you were within a toucher of departing this life. That you have lived is something for which you may thank these young people."

Mr. Richard grunted but looked as though thanks were

the furthest things from his mind. Ben tugged at Constable Wilkes's sleeve. "Sir," he said, "I wish to claim the reward—Judge Thomas spoke of a reward offered for the return of the runaway bond servant Patience Martin."

"So he did," said Mr. Wilkes. "But that you shall have to take up with Mr. Worth here, for he offered the reward. Ten pounds, was it not, sir?"

Mr. Richard's pale face took on a slight tinge of color. "Yes," he said in his weak voice. "But Samuel Wilkes, you know very well that I offered the money for some honest person who would return the girl to me and account for the money!"

Dr. Blackthorn said in an angry tone, "Richard Worth, do something for once in your life because it is right and not because it feeds your prejudicial, narrow idea of the world! You offered ten pounds for her capture and return, and here she stands before you! More, you now have an accounting for the missing money, though it is one not to your liking. By heaven, sir, if you do not make good on your word, I shall give the reward myself—and then charge you double that for trying to heal your sick soul as well as your ailing body!"

"I never said that I would not pay," growled Mr. Richard, though he glared most wickedly at me. He fumbled for his purse, and from its depths he grudgingly counted out shillings, one Spanish gold pistole, and some five-shilling notes, until the amount was made up. These he passed to the doctor, who then gave them to Ben.

"Thank you, sir," Ben said. He went through the money, keeping nearly all the notes himself and giving me almost all the coins, until he had divided the amount exactly in half. I admired the quickness of his counting, for he reckoned it all in his head. Then he counted out another sum, almost all in the paper notes, and held that out to Mr. Richard. "Sir," he said, "four pounds. I buy Patience Martin's indentures of you."

"That is naught but foolishness!" gasped the sick man.

"You had already sent to the *Courant* an advertisement to that effect when Patience had to run from you to avoid your wicked intent to sell her to a bad master," Ben said, as though he had written out and memorized the speech. "We have it yet in the printing office, written in your own hand, and I can show it to the magistrates. I give you the four pounds you require, sir, in exchange for the indentures of Patience Martin."

"Have sense, Richard," the doctor said. "If you do not agree, what will you do with the girl? I'll not see her misused, not when she has proven so enterprising and intelligent."

"Very well," growled Mr. Richard, shaking with barely repressed fury. "The paper is in the top desk drawer in my bedroom."

Constable Wilkes sent another man to ride for it, and he took Betty Thayer to let him into the house. The rider was back within half an hour, bearing my note of indenture. It was about ten inches by thirteen, folded four times. Ben accepted and opened it, and standing beside him, I could read the large heading: *This Indenture Witnesseth*. It was all in handwriting, and at the bottom it had been signed by my father and by Jared Worth. I felt a little cold. It was strange to think that this one sheet of paper, signed and sealed, held seven years of my life imprisoned in its words.

"This is in order," Ben said. He handed the paper to me. "I surrender the indentures to Patience Martin," he said boldly. "I renounce all claim to the document. 'Tis hers to do with as she pleases."

I hesitated for not more than a few heartbeats before tearing the paper in half, and those in half again.

"Fool of a girl," Mr. Richard said bitterly, glaring at me with open anger. "And now how are you to live, pray tell? What do you suppose is to become of you in this hard world?"

"I know not, sir," I told him, holding my head high.

"Only that whatever my fate and my future shall be, they shall come of my own making. Come, Ben."

We went across to the prison, where after a tedious long time all the words had been exchanged, all the decisions had been made, all the documents had been fair-copied, signed, and sealed, and at the end of it all Moll Bacon smiled at us. She was free to go.

In the bright light of a waxing moon, the hatchet-faced woman stood outside the prison house, her head inclined to one side, and studied Ben and me. "So you two have saved my life, have you?" she asked softly, sounding not so much grateful as simply pleased.

"We tried to discover the truth, ma'am," Ben said. "And in so doing we have set you free, at least. The Good Book says the truth shall make you free, you know."

"John, chapter eight, verse thirty-two. I am not a heathen, Master Franklin," replied Moll tartly, but with a smile. "Walk along to my home with me, you two. I want to be assured that no one has broken in whilst I was held in prison."

We went to Water Street. In the moonlight Moll's little house looked whole from the outside, still neat and trim, although the frost had withered all the herb and flower beds. And though its door had not been locked, when we lit the lamps we found no sign of anyone's intruding, save for the grimy footprints of the men who had searched in vain for poisons. They had left things in some disarray, and Moll clucked over the slovenliness of the men. "Well, I shall clean up after them tomorrow," she said.

Then she made tea, and we sat around her little table and drank it. "Now I will return to my midwifery," she said in a considering voice. "And Master Franklin will continue to practice the printer's trade with his brother. But what will become of you, Patience?"

"I have some money now," I said, showing her the abundance of coins Ben had given me as my share of the reward. "I do not know what I can do, short of hiring myself out as a servant. But if I choose to do that, I shall be paid, not merely housed and fed, kept like a working farm animal, like a horse or a mule."

"We could clean out the small loft up there," Moll said in a thoughtful voice. "It has a window of its own, there is plenty of room for a bed, and you have the money to buy one."

I blinked at her. "Stay here with you, do you mean? Oh, Moll, I couldn't. I'd be a burden—"

"You would not," Moll said decisively. "You would be my pupil and my assistant. There is sorrow in midwifery, Patience Martin. There are times when you know a patient will not deliver a child but indeed will die herself—such was the case with Mrs. Worth, alas—"

Ben cried out in surprise. "You knew she was being poisoned?"

Moll shook her head gravely. "I did not, for I have never studied such things. But I knew she was doomed. She was not carrying a child within her at all, but was suffering from an internal growth, a cancer. I had not yet found the heart to tell that to her when she died of the poison."

I bowed my head, grieved that in her illness I had not been kinder to Mrs. Worth, though she had never shown much goodwill toward me.

"But I was saying," continued Moll, "though you will find much sorrow in midwifery, you will also find much joy. There are few things more wonderful in this world than bringing a new healthy life into it, and seeing the mother's smiles and the father's happiness. Come, Patience, try it. You may like it and take to it, and then again you may not. But you are free to make up your own mind now, and you shall do as you wish. If you find the tasks unpleasant and unrewarding, you may go off in search of something that better pleases you; if you are happy in the work and in the learning, why, you may stay here with me as long as you like."

I thought it all over for a few minutes. Then I said, "I shall stay."

"I think we shall get on well, you and I," Moll said with a pleased nod. "You know, when I was only eighteen and married just a year to my late husband, I had a little baby girl. Sorrowfully, she died within the month, and I never had another. Now, I think, I shall know what it would have been like to have a daughter."

"I must leave," Ben said, standing up. "I thank you for the tea, ma'am. Patience, I wish you joy of your new home. Come to see me at the printing house now and again and tell me what 'tis like to be free of your indentures! Don't forget, for I fear that without you to get me in trouble, life will be dull. I hope that someday I will know the same happiness that you have found tonight."

I rose and gave him a quick, sisterly hug. "I am sure you will," I said. Despite my joy my throat grew tight, and tears threatened to flood my eyes as I added, "For I never knew a cleverer boy than you, Ben Franklin."

Looking for another intriguing historical mystery? Don't miss Bailey MacDonald's

Wicked Will.

Turn the page for a special preview!

The night before had shrieked with wind and boomed with thunder, but dawn broke rain-washed and cool. We strolling players had no inkling that another and much worse kind of storm lay ahead. Indeed, that June morning in 1576 struck us all as a good omen, fair weather following foul.

Since before sunrise our wagon had been rumbling along toward Stratford-on-Avon. Bright woolly clouds drifted across the sky like white sheep grazing the hills of high heaven. From the trees on either side of the road cuckoos sent their double calls floating on the air. Even when the sun stood directly overhead, the day felt cool for June, and the four members of our acting company who had to amble along behind the wagon, Watkyn Bishop, Peter Stonecypher, Alan Franklin, and Michael Moresby, did not complain, though to be sure by noon they had long since ceased to sing their jolly walking songs. The wagon, crammed with our costumes and properties, held only my uncle, Matthew Bailey, old Ben Fadger, and me.

Or it *had* held me, until a mile back on the road, when Uncle Matthew had taken up the local boy who called himself Will to be our guide. Nearly a year of acting had introduced me to audiences both rude and civil, made up of all sorts of people young and old, but the main point about audiences was that they usually listened more than they spoke. Such was not true of Will, and he wouldn't take my stubborn silences or irritated shrugs as answers to his questions.

The boy, who had a plain face under an untidy thatch of brown hair, began with, "I'm called Will. What's your name?"

I saw my uncle's red face twitch in a pleading wink, asking me to suffer this prying boy's curiosity.

"Thomas Pryne," I said, adding no more because I had no wish to encourage his chat.

But he would not take a hint. "How old are you?"

"Twelve," I said shortly. That was a lie, for I was within

days of turning fourteen, but 'twas a lie my uncle wanted me to tell.

"So am I! I was twelve this April past! You're small for twelve, are you not?"

I stared at him in astonished exasperation. What did he mean "small"? I was taller than he was, big enough to give a chattering boy a bloody nose, I thought silently—but I merely grunted.

"Where are your parents?" he then asked.

I turned my head away from him so he would not see the tears that stung my eyes. "Both dead," I replied, twisting the tail of my shirt hard in my hands and fighting the urge to weep. I am a player, used to pretending feelings I do not have and hiding those I do. Even so, my throat ached with grief.

Will had all the sensitivity of a tree stump. "How did they die?" he asked eagerly.

I gave my uncle a dark look: *See what you've got me into.* But I said to Will, "Plague." That dread word alone was usually enough to silence anyone.

Not Will, though. "We've had plague in town before. There's a charnel house next to the church crammed floor to ceiling with bones! I often think of the horrible ghosts that must haunt it! Did your parents die in London—?"

At that last question, I had leaped down from the wagon to walk alongside our mare, Molly, with the heart inside me tightening like a hand clutching a hard pebble of pain. If the pest of a boy could not ask me more questions, I would have to tell no more lies. Trust Matthew Bailey, that great laughing hulk of a man, to befriend an annoyance like Will. I was angry to my soul with my big, hearty, broad-faced uncle, so unlike his sister, my mother. She was a frail creature, and though I had claimed her dead of the plague, she was not so. At least I hoped she was not, nor my father, but for all I knew, both of them might have passed on and been buried anytime the past nine months, for I had heard nothing from them in all that time. If they still lived, I thought in despair, they must have forgotten me.

I quickly decided that this Stratford Will was a thick-skull, an ignorant fool. You might have supposed that my jumping down to get away from his flapping tongue would have embarrassed him and stilled his curiosity, but no. Will's jabber rang in my ears as, like Robin Hood launching arrows at a target, the boy loosed question after question at my uncle: What plays did we have by heart? Where would we act? Did we know that two years before, Queen Elizabeth herself had visited Kenilworth Castle, not far from Stratford? That Lord Leicester had produced for the queen a play in which a merman riding on a dolphin sang a song? Did we have fireworks? Those and a hundred other skimble-skamble inquiries barbed the air until at last even Uncle Matthew had his fill and checked young Will's chatter.

"Hold, enough! Your questions pelt me like raindrops; one has not soaked in before another falls!" My uncle's words were angry, but not his tone of voice. Indeed, he fairly chuckled as he spoke to Will, sitting beside him up there in my rightful place.

"I am truly sorry," Will said, though he did not sound sorry at all. "But you have been all over the kingdom! You have played before princes and rogues, you have stood on stages and on cobblestones, you have seen England from one end to the other—"

"And we have heard the chimes at midnight!" interrupted my uncle, laughing. He leaned and called down to me, "Tom, lad, don't be unfriendly, pray. Now be a good fellow and climb back up to sit beside Master Will and try to answer one or two of his questions. 'Tis not far to Stratford, but should I pause to answer Will myself, we would never get to our sleeping-place before we hear those midnight chimes again. Make way, Master Will!"

The wagon creaked to a halt, Dunce and Molly snorted

and stamped, and I heard old Ben Fadger swear at the change in motion. Ben perched on a great mound of things, for all we owned, from the lumber for our stage to the tents in which we sometimes slept, the properties and costumes and curtains and all, crammed the wagon to overflowing, and crowning the heap sat crickety, cursing old Ben. No matter how many times Uncle Matthew told him to wait for stillness and steadiness, Ben would always try to stitch up the rips and tears as the wagon wobbled along, and because of that he kept pricking the needle into his horny old fingers. He complained and swore, though no one listened to him much.

As I settled on the seat, Will pointed ahead. "Turn left at the post there, 'tis the nearest way. Did you know we have a fortnight's holiday from school? 'Tis lucky for you, for if you had come this time last week I'd have been hard at the Latin and could not have guided you. Do you really play the women's parts?"

"I do."

"You have a head of hair for it—such soft, golden curls! Do you often fool the audience?"

"I always do," I said.

"Tom's a good actor," put in my uncle. "So are we all, all good actors!"

I knew he was trying to distract Will, but the talkative boy took no notice and gabbled on: "There are but seven of you in all, and plays I have seen often have a dozen or more parts. Do you each take only one part, or do—?"

"Peace, you fast-flowing spring of words!" said my uncle with another easy laugh. "Peace, you hailstorm of questions! By my faith, young Will, you spout words as a whale spouts vapor, blasting them into the air and mystifying the whole neighborhood with the drops. Did you say the mayor's name is Richard Hill?"

Will nearly bounced on the hard seat in his eagerness to answer. "Aye, and a stout friend of my father's, if you need my father's good word. He was bailiff not long ago, and still is on the town council. Oh, I should tell you we don't call the town master the mayor in Stratford, but the bailiff. I— but keep to the other side of the way here, Master Bailey, or else we'll bring down the spite of Speight."

"The spite of spite?" I said, not understanding.

"The man's name is Speight," Will explained with a nervous grin. "Old Edmund Speight. He is a landowner and a miserable miser. These are his fields and, in good faith, I think he thinks the queen's high road is his, too. He—" Will broke off at the sound of raised voices and grimaced. "There he is now," he said, sounding alarmed if not outright frightened. Some distance ahead two men stood, and as we neared I heard them shouting at each other in anger. So full of fury they seemed that I thought they were on the point of striking out with fists—or with blades.